SOMEONE ELSE'S CASTLE

JH Tomen

For Buddy.
A castle in your own right, your ramparts I called home.

et tui amóris in eis ignem accénde
renovábis fáciem terræ

Editing by A.K. Edits (@AdotKEdits)
Cover by Karl Nilsson (@sigvardnilsson)*

*Cover includes portions of Beck's Castle Ruins by László Mednyánszky
Denbigh Castle, Wales by Edward Dayes & Paysage de la Grand Chartreuse
attributed to Jean Lubin Vauzelle

Clouds

Siveh lay on her back, looking up at the writing in the sky. Even if Mimu wasn't convinced — *"They're just steaming clouds, Siveh, don't be a child!"* — she knew what they were. They were *thoughts*, written in the air. They looked like clouds, sure — puffy, white, drifting across the sky — but they had too much to say to be random. Besides, her parents couldn't seem to see anything beyond their noses. Even when a real cloud came by, they never seemed to see the shapes she saw in them.

She quickly traced her finger through the thick line of words, trying to decipher them before they dissipated. Like an old man's beard, they were long and billowy, rising from the forest in a line. It reminded her of the scarves Mimu knitted in the winter, or the long lore weaves the priests wore on their backs, the words hidden in the looping yarn. Pipu had taught her to read a few years back — before he got too busy to do anything but mind the forge — though without money for word ropes, she wasn't the most practiced. Which only made the writing in the sky all the stranger...

After... River... Seven... Trees... Lost... Key...

The writing in the sky never repeated the same message — assuming she wasn't completely misreading it — but it always said *something* about the river. Where did it come from, though? And what did it mean? It stood to reason that the clouds came from a forge — only a giant one compared to what they had on the farm — but she could never see the writing on the days they were in town. She went with Pipu once a month for his deliveries, but there was nothing there. Just the inn and the castle up on the hill, same as always. She'd even walked to the river a few times, but it was always empty, the water rushing by as it had all her life.

"Siveh!" Mimu yelled from down the hill. "Get down here!"

She was hoping the giant tree would hide her, but it seemed Mimu knew she was up on the hill all the same. She picked up the spirit stone beside her, heading down the grassy slope. The tiny man-shaped rock was warm to the touch from sitting in the sun, and luckily, it was a big one. Pretending to look for them was the only reason her parents let her wander the farm in the first place. She hadn't told them, but she'd found a patch of stones just beyond the tree line, and it grew a new one two or three times a week. As long as there was a new stone, she could harvest it and spend the rest of the time watching the clouds.

Hopefully Mimu just wanted her to help in the garden. She didn't mind *that* work. Farming — the way the plants grew, when they wanted water and how much — was something she could understand. Besides, at the end, they got to eat what they'd grown, Mimu's stews capturing the flavor of all their hard work.

The only chore she truly hated was helping Pipu with the ci'ru forge — its purple glow, the searing heat, feeding it all the spirit stones they could find. What was the point of it all? Pipu worked day and night just for the privilege of keeping it on the farm. It kept them warm in winter, sure, but it didn't seem to make their lives any easier beyond that. Every bit of metal they made went to the tax collector, off to make some sword for the war that had driven them to the farm in the first place.

They didn't even seem to own the farm — at least from the way her parents argued about it when they thought she was sleeping. Sometimes, when she was mad, she told Mimu she missed their cottage in the city, but the truth was, she didn't really remember it. Even if the war ended, would they really go back there? Her parents always talked about how much better life was in the city — every kind of food, buildings everywhere. But all she wanted was her hill and her clouds. She wouldn't be a little girl forever, and when she was grown, she'd follow that writing in the sky.

"Why do you make me yell for you, girl?" Mimu said, waiting for her by the gate with her hands on her hips.

"I couldn't hear you."

"Sure, and I'm the king's wife. Your father's looking for you."

Siveh's heart sank. So it was to be the forge today. She hung her head, heading for the back of the house where the forge was set into the wall.

"And don't you drag those feet through my plants!" Mimu yelled, though she'd been doing just that.

The worst thing about parents wasn't the chores, it was that they expected you to smile about them.

As she came around the side of the house, she found Pipu kneeling beside the forge, his hand *inside* the bulbous metal beast. She stopped, her eyes widening. The forge was hot enough to melt stone, so why wasn't his hand already turned to ash? But there was no purple glow…no flame inside the forge. She'd pulled the stone from her apron, but Pipu just glanced at it, shaking his head.

"One of the rods broke, bloody thing. I told the priest the writing looked wrong, but you know how those bastards — er…*fools* — are."

The inside of the forge had twelve crystal rods, their surfaces etched with sacred glyphs. Pipu said the gods themselves gave the forge its flame, but if it broke, what did that mean for the gods' favor?

"I think we'll have to head into town to fix it, and I want you to come with me."

He muttered something about the priests and a little girl, but Siveh didn't care. She was already jumping around the back garden, every bit of dread and drudgery from her day wiped away. She *never* got to go to town outside of market days, and those were so far apart the wait might as well be forever. She took off around the side of the house again, eager to get her shawl before Pipu changed his mind.

Mimu was cooking in the kitchen, but she sprinted past her, climbing the curling stairs toward their bedroom. Like always, the room was unbearably hot, the odd dome-shaped house the king had given them always trapping the heat of the forge. She might not remember their house in the city, but there was no way it could have been this stifling. Mimu even said it had been near the sea, with windows that opened and everything.

"Siveh!" Mimu called. "You get out of the house this minute and help your poor Pipu!"

Siveh ran back down, her shawl in hand. Mimu was looking at the ceiling, signing to the gods with both thumbs on her chin.

"How was I cursed with such a daughter?" Mimu asked, though Siveh knew it wasn't really a prayer.

"I *am* helping Pipu," Siveh said, whipping her shawl around her shoulder like it was the king's own robe. "He says we have to go to town, the forge is broke."

"Broken," Mimu corrected, clucking her tongue. "And we'll see about that."

She stomped toward the garden — no doubt trying to keep them from leaving the farm — but Siveh darted around her, beating her outside. Ever since the war had started, Mimu was terrified of everything off the farm, but there was no way she could keep them here today. The forges were the only things that truly mattered in this town, and Pipu would stop at nothing to fix his. Besides, there was never any writing in the sky on market days. If she was ever going to investigate what was really going on in town, it would have to be today.

Pipu already had the wagon out, hitching the kornaes to their harness. The three giant birds were restless, kicking at the dirt with their claws, though they perked up when they saw Siveh. She reached into her pocket for the clump of flowers she'd picked, giggling as the scratchy bird tongues danced around her palm. Her parents argued for a few minutes, but she ignored them, leading the birds toward the gate. Usually, Mimu won their fights, but she knew what the result would be when the forge was involved.

Pipu climbed up next to Siveh on the wagon, giving her his usual sad smile as he urged the kornaes forward, turning into the forest toward the castle road. Pipu tried to talk to her as he drove, but she could hardly pay him any mind. After an endless supply of boring days, *this* was something new. For once, she had a chance to see something special, and she wouldn't miss it for anything. Even if there would be a mountain of chores waiting for her when they got back, she wanted to savor this.

She kept looking at the sky, squinting through the canopy, but it was impossible to make out any of the words. Still, she could tell they were there, and that was reassurance enough. Like the gods' own hands, they beckoned to her, waving her toward the castle and a lifetime of secrets she'd been begging the world to tell her.

Finally, she began to smell smoke, and before long, she could *hear* the castle, the murmur of voices and the clanging of metal carrying through the forest. As they cleared the trees, they came face to face with the Old Man, the giant spirit stone guarding the bridge into town. Bigger than their cottage, his eyes never left the sky, his entire face leaning back as his beard trailed into the river. The locals said it was the spirit of the river itself, the stone growing since before people had lived there. But that would have to be hundreds of years! If her patch of stones produced a man the size of her fist every week... Well, this one must have been growing for more years than she could count.

The castle was built on an island where the river split, its gates opening onto narrow bridges on every side but the one where the town sat. No one seemed to mind being surrounded by water, though, and the houses were all built like tall, spindly birds wandering the river for fish. It reminded her of the city, actually, even if she only had vague memories of the place. Still, she could remember buildings looming over her, though the village must have been tiny by comparison.

They passed the bakery and the fishmonger, crossing the central square to the back half of the village where the army had taken over everything. Farriers were working on horses and men in plate crisscrossed the cobblestones, each of them wearing a sword that was longer than she was tall. The smithy, though, was the busiest of all, choking with villagers who had come to get supplies for their ci'ru forges, the purple light glowing against their faces.

Siveh perked up as Pipu parked the cart. The smithy didn't run its forge on market days, the one day of the week the soldiers took off their armor and stopped looking like metal bugs — even though Mimu forced them to come home before dark when "the men become beasts," whatever that meant. Still, as she followed the smithy's smoke into the sky, it didn't seem to be the source of the clouds. It was like Pipu's forge, just plain, old, boring smoke.

She sighed, looking at the clouds again. Was this a waste of time after all? Maybe the clouds were coming from somewhere different altogether, a place—

The castle.

Her eyes widened, tracing the letters down from the sky and into the king's keep. Was there a forge hidden inside? One she'd never heard about?

"I have to get in line," Pipu said, holding the broken rod from the forge. "Can I trust you to be good, or do I need to make you wait with me?"

"I'll be good, promise," she said quickly, crossing her heart. Still, she didn't wait for Pipu to change his mind, jumping off the cart as she hurried across the square. She didn't head straight for the castle, of course. She was old enough to know Pipu always watched her longer than she thought, and it wasn't like the guards would let her get close anyway. Only a fool got too close to the soldiers, like Tifal, the innkeeper's boy who'd lost his hand that spring. She headed for the riverbank instead, crossing in between the houses as if she were looking for tadpoles like she usually did.

She went up to the retaining wall, climbing over it as she dropped a few feet into the reeds at the water's edge. It was the perfect way to reach the bridge under the castle. It was certainly a place she'd guard if she were king, but just like her parents with the clouds, it seemed all adults were keen on ignoring anything that didn't fit their perfect vision of the world.

She moved quickly, afraid she wouldn't be able to hear Pipu calling her name by the water. As she reached the bridge, though, she froze, making out the shape of a person in the darkness. They knelt by the water, pouring out a shiny liquid from a bottle. Someone from the palace?

Someone who would call for guards? Maybe she was the fool, after all…
She moved backward, hoping to sneak back over the wall, when a reed
cracked beneath her foot. The person's head shot up, their eyes as wide
as the moon. It was…a girl.

"Who sent you?" the girl asked, pulling a knife as she stood, tucking
away the bottle.

"N-no one," Siveh stammered, putting her hands up. "Promise. I only
wanted to see about the clouds."

"The clouds?" the girl asked, cocking her head. Her hair seemed to
shine in the darkness, her braids choking with gold and set with a diadem.

"Are you…the princess?"

"Never mind that," the other girl said, kneeling by the water again. "If
you can see the clouds, you can't be all bad, but either help me or leave
— before you get us both caught."

Siveh wandered over, standing by the girl's side as she took out
another bottle. She motioned for Siveh to crouch too, handing it to her.
The bottle was no bigger than her palm, made of glass the color of
midnight. It seemed to pulse in her hand, like it had a heartbeat.

"Pour it in," the girl said, motioning for Siveh to copy her. "Slowly,
mind you."

Siveh poured her bottle into the burbling water. Where the other girl's
was rainbow, hers was silver, like moonlight. It poured like honey,
though it seemed to glimmer for a moment in the darkness, like there
were words written on its surface.

"Are you…*making* the clouds?"

"Someone has to," the girl said, though she eyed Siveh, weighing her.
"The smithy only fixes swords. The real forge is inside the castle, and it
sucks up water from the river." She motioned behind her, where the
water roared as it pushed through a grate in the castle's base. "If you put
the words in the water, they come out as clouds."

"I've seen them from my farm. But what do they mean? The words
always mention the river, but I didn't understand the rest."

The girl sighed, taking the bottle back from Siveh and handing her
another one.

"I guess I'm lucky you could read that much. Cloud writing is part of
the old magic, the kind my mother taught me. No one takes it seriously,
of course — which I guess is good since I've gone this long without
getting caught — but I'm looking for a magician, someone who can stop
my father."

"Your…father? The king?"

"Yes," the girl said, her face growing hard as she stared into the water.

It was the same look Mimu sometimes wore when she thought Siveh wasn't looking, staring out the garden window. "These swords are an abomination. They harvest souls in his foolish war, forcing them back here as spirit stones. More stones, more swords; the cycle never ends."

Siveh's mouth fell open, nearly dropping her bottle in the river — though it earned her a glare from the other girl. Still, could such an awful thing be true? She'd been harvesting the spirit stones for years, her parents tossing them in the forge like firewood. Were they really…souls?

"So, you're just like the others, eh?" the girl asked. "Convinced this war is worth fighting, working away at your forge?"

"I hate the forge."

The girl nodded evenly, the first time she'd shown Siveh even a glimmer of respect.

"But you said your mother taught you, right? If the queen is in the castle too, why doesn't she—"

"That woman isn't my mother," the other girl spat. "Father just stores us here. But when the magician comes, I'll get out of here and see about my revenge."

Siveh had thought she'd had it hard, skirting her chores on the farm, every day the same as the last. But this girl couldn't even trust her own mother — or the woman married to her father, anyway. Was Mimu right, that the castle was full of snakes? But what of them? If what this girl said was true, and every stone in their forge was another stolen soul… What had happened back in the city? Why had they really left?

"Where's your farm?" the other girl asked, eyeing Siveh as she took back the bottle.

"To the south, just inside the forest."

"Toward the capital… Would you help me if you could?"

Siveh nodded. How could she not? After all these months of watching clouds, how could she ever just go back to farming?

The other girl pulled a necklace from under her dress. It looked like gold, the delicate chain holding a tiny metal vial no bigger than a thimble.

"This is my reserve, in case I ever get caught. I make it with chips from the Old Man. It's just one word, but it's the name of this place, and if your clouds get further than mine…"

Siveh took the vial in her hand, holding her breath as she stared at it. Even more than the bigger bottle, it was like she could feel the cloud inside, hearing the word in her mind as she held its power.

"Put one drop in your father's forge each night when he's asleep. It should last the entire month. If nothing happens by then, come to the market and I'll give you more."

Siveh nodded, though this suddenly all felt like a dream.

"You should go," the other girl said, taking the necklace from her palm and putting it around Siveh's neck. "And so should I." She stood, looking up at the bridge. She walked over to the stone retaining wall and, with a push, opened a hidden door in the base of the castle.

"Thank you," she said, finally smiling. "Hope can be dangerous, but I think you've given me some today."

She shut the door behind her, never asking for Siveh's name nor giving up her own. She could feel the necklace thrumming against her chest, warming her skin as it boiled with power.

"Siveh!" she heard Pipu call, waking her from her dream.

Had he been calling long? She dashed back through the reeds and over the retaining wall. Pipu was standing in the middle of the square, a new rod in hand and an angry look on his face. Still, she didn't even feel afraid. After all, what was a few extra chores compared to *magic?* For the first time in her life, she had work of her own, something only she could do. It wasn't enough to dream of clouds written in the sky. It was time to write them.

The King

My father was king of these lands, a giant. I grew up surrounded by feasting and the sound of horns, the stones of his throne room my crib. But I knew the ramparts of his castle best, waiting for his banner to return after battle, the golden lion fluttering over the hills. And return it always did. His arm never tired, and his head never swayed, his proud knights knowing only victory. Instead, it was I who left these lands, sent by his own hand and for my own good. No pampered princeling I, he sent me to the hinterlands to live a simpler life, to know the truth of what — and *who* — a kingdom is.

My father was a good man, a noble man. But as I rode back south, the trees swaying in a wind that smelled of smoke, you could hardly tell these lands had once been his. But I suppose the two were intertwined — our kingdom's prosperity and its undoing. My father had built many mines, scouring the earth for riches. He was a generous man, raining gold on every farm, but the mines had dug too deep. They woke dragons our songs had never named, born as if from the stones themselves, our swords and arrows useless against their skin.

Still, I didn't blame my father. The world was different then, split into before and after, the consequences hidden until far too late. I only wished I had his boldness, his strength. Even as I rode home, I knew I was only a shadow to his colossus. I was a listener, a watcher on the wall, sure of his greatness even as it slipped through my hands. I'd spent my life afraid I'd destroy what he had built. How, then, was I to rebuild his world without him?

"Looks like a Jade Shard's been this way," Här said from behind me.

As we left the tree line, a wide valley stretched before us, dotted with hills. The closest one had been scorched black, the windmill set atop it left only with a few jagged stones at its base. We'd spoken of nothing but dragons since riding out from Hinnespur. There was much for me to learn, of course, about these new creatures, but I also suspected it was partly to keep from talking of other, heavier things.

There was a...*weight* to Här I'd never seen before, the giant man bowed by his burdens. He'd fled the coup on my father's orders to bring me back south. Loyal to the end, he probably wished he'd died by my father's side, but surely there had been enough dying. Even the men who'd killed my father had merely been afraid, desperate to cling to what little remained of their world. They had loved my father, hadn't they? Even if they were oath breakers, I had to believe there was a way back. But that was a problem for another day. Until we dealt with the dragons, what point was there in holding a castle?

"How can you tell?" I asked Här, stopping my horse so we could look out at the valley.

"It's the way the fire stretches," he said, pointing to the east where other hillsides had been burnt. "They fly low to the ground, spitting fire every hundred yards."

Even as the damage stretched for miles, it was nothing compared to the wreckage we'd seen in Elifor, where a Sapphire Heart had destroyed the entire village, its fire dropping down from on high like lightning as it cratered the earth. There were at least a half-dozen different types of dragons, each one with its own unique flavor of destruction.

"Think it's still around?"

"Not likely, my lord," Här said, scanning the horizon. "Grass would still be burning. Once a Jade Shard starts a line, they just keep going. Like they're *drawing* something."

It wasn't exactly reassuring that the dragons could be drawing thalograms — or worse — on our lands, but what was one more terror?

"I'm not a lord anymore, Här," I said, nudging my horse forward again.

"You will be if I have anything to say about it," he said, following behind, his hand on his sword — as if he'd have time to draw it if a dragon found us. "A kingdom's more than a throne, lad."

"That it is," I said, sighing. "How about you and I draw lots for the crown when this is over?"

Här laughed.

"See? That's why it's gotta be you. Your father spoke the same way. Besides, you're the one what learned the magic up north. But if either of us is still standing when this is over, I promise I'll at least wrestle you for it."

I shook my head, chuckling. Still, my mind lingered on his words. My father had spoken the same way? Of someone else being king? To me, he'd always been a mountain of confidence. But suppose he'd had his own doubts? He'd always worked himself harder than any of his liege lords — late nights reading letters, scouring maps and battle plans. Who could possibly have been a better fit for the throne than him? Certainly not me, and not with the paltry magic I *had* learned.

"I'm not sure I learned much of any use," I said, pulling my horse back onto the path as she reached for a low-hanging leaf. She was an old mare we'd picked up in Hinnespur. She wasn't trained like Här's warhorse, but she was sweet, and I'd taken a shine to her.

"The Ice Witch let me watch her ceremonies, but you heard her when we left. If we don't find at least a dozen witches down here, we've no chance of breaking through that dragon skin."

"Bloody stuck-up broken half-tooth of a—" Här muttered to himself. He hadn't taken kindly to the witch's refusal to join us, but who could blame her? The treaty with Hinnespur had been signed by my father, and his kingdom was a heap of ash. What could she possibly gain by helping us take it back?

"We'll find the witches," I said, ignoring some of the choicer words he'd used to describe my mentor. "Besides, it's what we need. We lost our bond to the land somehow, and these women still have one. We're not just slaying dragons, Här, we're begging the gods for mercy."

"That's why you're in charge, my lord," Här said, laughing. "I'm just an angry old hammer looking for a nail. Be right back."

He pushed ahead, riding his horse to the top of the next rise. He always insisted on taking the front guard when we couldn't see what was ahead, even though I kept asking him not to. I'd be hopeless without him, so what was the point of putting himself in danger?

Just as quickly, though, I heard his horse again. He rode hard back over the hill, barely reining in as he reached me, his face ashen.

"What is it?"

He licked his lips under his helm, shaking his head.

"There's a house, my lord, smoke coming from the chimney."

"Well, that's great," I said, straining to see over the hill. I hadn't noticed the smoke amidst all the dragon burns, but if someone had survived the attack…

"That's just it, my lord. There was nothing here when I rode north. This place is new, but it looks a hundred years old at least."

"Then it's exactly what we need."

I galloped up the hill, already knowing what I'd find. There, in the middle of a field of ash, was a stone witch's hut. Shaped like a cone, it was made of interlocking rocks, each one carved with a glyph. A place like this would take a group of men two years to build, but a stone witch didn't need such time. She simply moved where she pleased, calling on the bedrock to rebuild her home when she arrived.

"What did I tell you?" I asked Här, grinning as he caught up. "Twelve witches is nothing."

"My lord," he whispered, "maybe—"

But I was already off, riding toward the hut with a vengeance. Maybe it was familiarity that drove me forward — my time with the Ice Witch making me more comfortable around magic than any mortal ought to be — but as I placed my hand on the door, I realized I should have been more careful. The moment I touched it, my arm seized up, the muscles locking in place as if I'd been turned to stone.

Här was right behind me, and I waved him back with my good arm, trying to hide my malady before he pulled his sword. Excellent fighter that he was, his strength would be useless against a stone witch. Besides, my father had given him that sword, and I would have hated for it to be turned to dust in his hands. I closed my eyes, reaching for what tiny magic I had inside me. Still, it was barely a whisper, my distance from Hinnespur straining my connection. I thought I'd have time to reconnect to my homeland, to transfer my abilities here, to…show my father what I'd learned.

Before I could grasp my spark of power, however, I heard the door creak open, my arm suddenly free of its bonds. It was dark inside the hut, but in the soft glow of a fire burned down to the embers — completely at odds with the column of smoke outside — I saw the outline of a woman.

"So, it's a prince who sees fit to seize my door."

Before I could speak, the doorway seemed to *tilt,* the earth itself changing beneath our feet, the newly formed ramp forcing us into the entryway and into a smoldering heat. My throat was suddenly dry, but I fought the urge to cough. If she was going to help us, the next few moments would be essential. Luckily, I'd learned the hard way in Hinnespur that the only qualities every witch admired were modesty and curiosity.

"You knew I was the prince?" I asked, grateful Här still had his arm at his side.

"Knowing, not knowing, is there a difference to the earth?"

As my eyes adjusted, I could finally make out her face. Her eyes were milky with age, but she looked young otherwise — young enough to be my sister — her hair silken like she'd only just brushed it. Between us was an urn. It sat inside the fire, reaching to her chest. It was cracked in dozens of places, though the cracks almost seemed to move, shining in the glow of the fire. Was it a trick of the eye? Some magic? The witches in Hinnespur often wrote in ice, but this woman seemed completely still, at odds with the effort I knew such magic took.

"I suppose not," I said carefully, "though I'd think the earth sees a great deal in these lands. Do you know why I've come?"

She chuckled.

"I know why you *think* you've come," she said, gesturing toward the urn in the fire. "You see the dragons as an aberration, as something separate from these lands. But tell me — if a Sapphire Heart doesn't belong in the air, then why is it the color of the sky? Take the one you saw down south. Even now, it dances with the earth, moving with the rhythms of the others. Do you know any beast like that?"

I looked closer, finally noticing the color of the cracks in the urn. The one nearest me was a bright blue. It traced its way toward the bottom of the base, intersecting with the others circling around the vase. There were pockets where the crack grew larger, forming a perfect circle before it continued…just like the crater I saw the Sapphire Heart dig into the earth.

"This…is the world? Our world?"

"Part of it," the witch answered as she stood. Här tensed behind me, but I opened my palm, urging him to be still. She was silent as she moved, the stones seeming to swallow her footsteps as she approached the urn. She met my eyes as she traced the cracks absently with a long, delicate finger, her fingernail a deep black like it had been burned. "There is a limit to how far any soul can see, but as I said, the earth knows much in its unknowing. Take you, for instance. I can see your cracks, the truth of how you were made."

I opened my mouth but couldn't seem to speak. Something about what she said brought Father into my mind, though out of memory or magic I wasn't sure. I could picture him on our walks growing up, when he would take me to look at the fish in the castle stream. There was something he'd said once — "a man may be a shield, but he's only as strong as his cracks."

"Did you know my father? I'm afraid I have more cracks than he. I'm not sure I'm fit for the task he left behind."

"Perhaps, but all men have their cracks, their weakness. It was your father's weakness that made him stronger. So will yours if you let it. Take the dragons — they crack the earth not to destroy it, but to make it new. If your brokenness allows you to see that truth, then maybe you are every bit as strong as he."

"And let them kill whoever they like?" Här spat, unable to contain himself any longer.

The witch moved in the span of a breath, impossibly fast as she reached Här, staring into his eyes as she pointed at his chest, seemingly unafraid of his hulking frame.

"It was man betrayed the earth, boy. Long before the mines, the forges dumping slag into the rivers. You thought man could live without the Mother's grace? You thought she would sit forever, never rising to defend herself?"

"I…I'm sorry," Här said, bowing his head, though it seemed he meant it more for me than her.

The witch chuckled, patting his cheek.

"You are forgiven. After all, the Great Mother bade you to defend yourself as well. But—" she added, turning to face me, her hands behind her back. "I know the question you want to ask of me, child, to join your cause. I may well help you, but know this — I refuse to serve the Mother's enemies. There is no justice in it — and no point. You will fail if you fight the dragons. But if you *serve* her, make an offering — a *true* offering — you may prevail yet. These are my terms. If you seek to save the earth, not as it was but as it should be, then I'll take you to the others."

The others. I glanced at Här, taking a deep breath. It was almost an impossible amount of information to take in, but something about what she said made sense. The dragons hadn't escaped the earth; they *were* the earth. How else could the beasts have such power? More importantly, it hadn't taken long for me to realize how useless our resistance was. I wasn't sure what kind of offering they would demand, but I would make it, especially if the cost came from me and not my people. I would pay a thousand times. My father had never lost a war, but his son, weak as I was, could at least sue for peace.

"I ride with you, Good Witch — if you'll have us. Teach me of this offering, and I vow I'll do everything in my power to provide it."

"It seems you've already begun," she said, tapping the urn as she crossed the room.

I turned to look, the bright blue line suddenly vanishing. Its crack remained, but the light disappeared even though others kept moving across the stone.

The witch shooed us out, moving deeper into the hut.

"Give me a moment to pack my things!"

"See?" Här said, finally smiling as we stepped outside — though he still flexed his hand as if he wished his sword was in it. "You *are* like your father. It was people what mattered to him, not victories. You don't win a battle without people at your back."

"I hope so," I said, looking up at the sky. In some ways, it felt like I understood less than when I'd entered the hut, though as the Ice Witch said, that also meant I was closer to something of real value.

For a moment, I could see only darkness in the doorway, the sun blinding after the dim of the witch's hearth. Finally, she appeared, stepping through the entrance as the hut collapsed around her, swallowed into the earth with a groan.

"I ride with you, prince," she said, taking my arm as I walked her to the horse. She felt too light, frail even, like she had the bones of a bird. But for the first time in weeks, I felt solid, like I might actually save my people — even if that meant saving them from themselves… Still, I held onto that image of my father, sure he'd see us through. Perhaps it was his greatness — and its excess — that had brought the dragons, but it was the same greatness that would see us to the other side, holding us together as a people.

We rode south, putting the burnt field behind us, and for the first time since Hinnespur, I didn't watch the sky with fear.

Gardens

Siraf glanced out the window again, comparing the cloud outside to the one on her sketch pad. It was a massive thing, like a castle in the sky and—

And it was already blowing away. She went back to her sketch pad, finishing off the curl at the end. It wasn't exactly right, but it didn't matter, either. There would be another one right behind it, a battalion of shapes riding in on the breeze. Besides, clouds were fun to draw precisely because they took whatever shape you wanted. Even the biggest looked like you could draw them yourself — if only your brush could reach the sky.

Satisfied for the moment, she got up from her desk and plopped down on the thick cushion set into the bay window. While the desk was better for drawing, the window was better for watching, and she stared up at the mass of clouds, feeling like she might fall upwards into them if she stared long enough. She sighed, closing her eyes as she imagined she was floating.

"Perfect," she whispered to herself, smiling with her eyes closed.

The best days were the ones where you felt like a cloud, floating at your own pace and drifting wherever you chose. The others thought her silly for choosing the cottage, but where they saw dull afternoons, she saw only bliss. The queen's castle may have fashion and intrigue, but it was wanting for leisure. This was *her* castle, made only of gardens and clouds. Speaking of which…

Siraf cracked one eye open, looking out at the garden. She was technically meant to be minding the chayr plants, but being magic themselves, it wasn't like they needed much. Their roots refused water from anyone who wasn't a witch — which was why the guild had to pay someone to be here in the first place — but other than their daily watering, there wasn't much to do but measure their growth and jot down her notes. In short, it was the perfect job. After all, what was the point of magic if you had to work all the time? Like her mother always said, if the goddess only wanted men to toil, she wouldn't have given them smiles.

It was a nice thought, even if it made her wonder what they'd been given tears for… She got up, grabbing her notebook as she headed through the open door. The chayr plants were arranged in a figure eight, twenty of them in all. The long green stalks were already waist-high, and the grains floating around the ends were shaping themselves into copies of the clouds above. As she approached, though, the grains buzzed, reassembling themselves into twenty perfect copies of her face.

"Hello to you too," she said, laughing.

What the queen wanted with magical plants like these was anyone's guess, but she was happy to grow them. She'd only been at the cottage a month when they started copying her face. No one had mentioned that in previous reports, so hopefully, that meant they liked her… She knelt down by the one closest to the door, running her hand along its central stalk as the plant purred.

"You having a good day too?" she asked, reaching into her pocket for her measuring tape. Made of cloth, it was like Mama's dressmaking tape, only covered in magical sigils, measuring far more than length alone.

She measured the plants every which way, taking notes as she went. They were fairly uniform in length, but their magical properties seemed higher near the center. The shape of the figure eight was probably pulling in one of the goddess's essences from the fields, though it would take a priestess to know which one. She made a note for her report, though the flunkies in the castle never seemed to care about things like that. All they cared about was how quickly the plants grew.

She only hoped the queen didn't do something *boring* with them. In the castle, everything was a weapon, every piece of steel fit for a blade. But these plants were proof that they were wrong. Nothing magical ever grew in the castle's gardens, the plants suffocated by the never-ending slog of days meant only for working. Time wasn't meant to be clay, split into perfect little pieces of usefulness. Time was a river, meant to wash away all the falseness you'd buried your heart under. She was really beginning to sound like Mama — even in her head — but if they were only meant to work, why did the goddess make days and nights, summers and winters? The world itself needed rest, and so did they.

Siraf finished her measurements, flopping onto her back on the warm soil. Looking up at the sky, she could see the plants from the corner of her eye, adjusting their shape into the form of a resting woman. But it didn't look like her…it looked like Mama.

"Now you lot know I don't look anything like that!" she protested, propping herself up on one elbow to face the plants. The grains chittered, the shapes buzzing as if they were laughing. It seemed these plants read thoughts too… She decided not to put that in her notebook, though. Let the queen find out what she'd grown when her wicked thoughts were broadcast to the whole court.

She sighed, lying back down as a weight came over her. It still pained her that she couldn't change things at the castle. She'd tried when she was a novice, but in the end, the head witch had put her in her place just like she'd done to Mama twenty years ago. She felt a tear come to her eye, but was she crying for Mama or for wasting such a perfect day? She couldn't save the whole world, but she was still meant to save this time — this *place* — for herself.

Just then, the plant nearest to her head leaned over, its floating grains blocking the sky. They formed themselves into Mama's face, a ghostly hand of grain reaching out to touch her.

"Thank you," Siraf said, smiling sadly as she patted the plant's stalk in return. As the plant pointed itself back toward the sun, she found herself feeling better. Even though it hadn't really been Mama, she heard the woman's voice more clearly in her mind.

"Come, child, a bit of rain can't put out the sun."

She was being too hard on herself again, trying to prove she was grateful by clinging to every good thing. She *was* grateful, of course, but gratitude wasn't a stick to beat yourself over the head with. Even good days weren't meant to be just one thing. Like the seasons, the goddess had made life with sun *and* rain, and she wouldn't blame you for noticing both. A perfect day wasn't made with smiles, it was made by noticing what the world had to show you.

That being said, a perfect day *did* have tea… Sarif sat up, about to head to the kitchen when the plants all rearranged their grains into the shape of teacups. Just like the cottage's creaky cupboards, though, no two were alike. One even looked like her favorite heart-shaped mug, a chip missing from the lip…

"Is my tea time that predictable?" she asked, laughing as she stepped over the plants.

As the water boiled, she collected her tea leaves from their pots on the windowsill, humming to herself as she picked bits of flowers and herbs. It was Mama's old recipe — or close to it — and it always calmed her. Skydrop petals for her nerves, witch's tongue to ease her stomach, and cat's eye to brighten her dreams. Life was simply better when you made your own tea, which was just another thing to love about the cottage. In the castle, they only got a quarter-hour for tea, the murky stuff more like lukewarm lake water as it poured out of the rusted kettles.

Everyone in charge there seemed to think people were like eggs — needing cracking and boiling to be useful. But in reality, people weren't so different from the chayr plants. Give them what they needed — and leave them alone — and something *amazing* might happen.

With her tea made and the heart-shaped mug in hand, Siraf went back outside. As she reached the figure eight, though, she discovered something new. The grains had all shaped themselves into perfect circles, spinning around giant seeds that had appeared atop the stalks. Twice the size of acorns with skin that shimmered in the sun, they certainly hadn't been in her instructions…

She took one in her hand, the grains shifting into the shape of a hand planting the seed. Did they…want her to make more? She looked out at the horizon — as if the head witch would be stomping down the road to chide her — but there was nothing but clouds as far as the eye could see. They'd said someone would be by in a week or so to collect the plants, but if she planted new ones, they wouldn't need to go to the castle. In fact, they wouldn't need to do anything at all. They could grow here, drinking in the sun and drawing clouds. They could…be *free*.

Little Lights

I walked slowly through the forest, my eyes closed, feeling the connection with each tree before I moved on. I could sense the castle's many eyes over my shoulder — I was the most visible I'd been all year with the leaves falling — but it couldn't be helped. At least I'd worn my simplest dress, giving me a chance of blending in. Someone might tell the captain I was out here, but if I was going to be collecting light, I had to do it properly. Unfortunately, even in this "refuge" from the war, I could already sense how badly my light would be needed.

Take the captain. The mass of shadows hadn't reached this far north yet, but I could see one growing on his shoulder. I told no one, of course. The captain was beloved, and he was a good man as far as captains go — a bit *too* noble, perhaps, which few realized was how the shadows most often got in.

Everyone in the castle was a refugee in one way or another. They'd all seen the cities fall, had fled for their lives, but they still didn't understand. They saw the shadows as monsters, as something outside themselves. But every single one of the beasts had been a person once, their souls corrupted. The mind was like a castle. Each one had a gate, a courtyard full of light, but they all had dungeons and tunnels too. If you only looked above, you'd never see the darkness creeping in.

I heard the caw of a crow and opened my eyes, seeing three of my new friends circling in the sky. Storing the light I'd already collected in my mind, I reached into my pocket for a handful of seed. Holding it out at arm's length, the crows swooped down, landing on the forest floor.

"Hello, friends," I said as they hopped about, turning their heads this way and that to look at me. I knew one of them, *Gi'fan* — which meant something like 'old one' in the crow tongue — but the other two were new. It seemed *Gi'fan* was still keen on helping my cause, at least. There were at least a dozen in the murder seeking light in my name, but there were thousands more crows in the mountains to recruit — and thousands of places I'd never have time to reach on my own.

"Come, *Gi'fan,*" I said, gesturing with the seed, "show your friends how it's done."

With a flap of his wings, he sprang up onto my arm, burying his head in the pile of seed. I scratched his feathers as he ate, his beak cool against my palm. The other crows began to circle me, clearly eager for their turn. When *Gi'fan* was done, he turned to me, letting out a cheerful caw.

"Go on," I said, tapping my head. "Let me have a look."

He leapt up, my eyes going blank the moment his talons reached my hair. Suddenly, I saw a waterfall. The view was distorted, warped by the crow's eyes, but it seemed like one I remembered from when I was a child. I think they called it Heron's Tears, the water bluer than blue as it poured over the cliffs. I sucked in a breath, my mind returning to me, but not before the light *Gi'fan* had collected burrowed into my heart, adding its power to the rest.

"Well done," I said, reaching into another pocket for a piece of apple, which I tossed up to the bird. I scattered some seed for the others, and they flew off with *Gi'fan,* hopefully properly incentivized to join the search.

How long had it been since I'd seen that waterfall? Fifteen years? Twenty? I'd been no more than nine when the king had driven us out of our lands and into the city. How fitting — when it wasn't devastating — that these lands would become one of the last bastions of the kingdom's light. And even then, it was a matter of time before they stopped me from collecting it. "Witchcraft," they called it, even if it was their last hope. They probably wouldn't have even let me come north with the other refugees if I hadn't cut my hair, removing any sign I was from these sacred lands. Meanwhile, no one else at the castle likely even knew there were waterfalls to the north, the treasures of this place hidden to them.

I moved on, reconnecting with the trees as I wandered into the next glade. There was a stream running there, and I slipped my boots off, dipping in my toes. It was cold but full of light, thankfully bringing down new energy from the mountains despite my harvest here the week before. I crossed the water, boots in hand, to look at a new patch of whisper-loves that had just blossomed, their pink petals bursting with power.

"Thank you, little ones," I whispered as I caressed them, their memories coming into my mind. It was a brief thing, but they still remembered being seeds, the light coming in through their roots. They wouldn't live much longer with winter right around the corner, but there was glory in that too. Fall flowers leaping from the ground in the sliver of time given to them, intent on filling the forest with color even as the leaves fell.

I was starting to reach the most my heart could carry, but I pressed on, eager to have my fill before the sun set. Unfortunately, facing the shadow wasn't like preparing for winter. I couldn't divide my food by the days until spring, knowing when I had enough. Measuring light was a fragile thing — something my mother had barely understood herself — and there was no telling what the need would be besides. If Tu'resant fell to the south, we'd have untold refugees heading our way — with monsters on their heels — not to mention the shadows we had brewing in our midst.

I harvested one last giant oak and slipped my boots back on, heading for the castle. I didn't mind getting locked out when the gate shut for the evening — there was nothing willing to hurt me in this forest — but sleeping outside wouldn't help my fragile reputation. Even having cut my hair, the others could tell I was different, and it was only a matter of time before my plans were put at risk. The others were simple folk, content to work the fields, hiding from the darkness with their gruel and ale. But if they decided I seemed too much like a soul witch — or even worse, a bone seeker — they might not even send me from the castle alive.

As I made it back to the wall, the sun was almost to the trees, the half-dozen guards who lowered the gate each night already standing at their stations. The captain was with them, and as I stopped to curtsy, he fell in beside me.

"Taking another walk, *Feyhr* Sarin?" he asked.

He *was* honorable in his way, trying to use the proper title for each refugee's country — even if I wasn't really from the south. Still, he wasn't from the north either, and with my hair cut, it was plenty respectful considering.

"I was, Lord Captain," I said, smiling. "It's a lovely evening."

I looked over his left shoulder, where I could just make out the shadow peeking out from behind his epaulets. It looked like a worm, only you could see through it, the castle wall behind shimmering through its dark haze. It was still only about six inches long, but it was growing wider, and soon, it would spread down to his heart. Still, he *was* a good man. I only hoped I'd still be here to heal him when the time came — even if that meant he could never be a captain again.

"Well, my dear *Feyhr,* I only hope you'll be more careful. It can be dangerous outside the castle, and the others get nervous when they see you going out. The gods of plenty forbid you ever didn't make it back…"

He let the end trail off, leaving the most important part unsaid. The gods of plenty forbid I came back *changed,* a shadow on my back. Unfortunately, that wasn't how it worked. The shadows were everywhere, like spores, only growing where they found a fertile host. In my state, open to the light as I was, a shadow could kill me, true, but it wouldn't be able to tolerate wearing my skin.

"There's danger everywhere, Lord Captain," I said, "gods preserve us."

"Well, at least stay close where there's someone to protect you."

I simply smiled, bowing my head. He wasn't exactly barring me from the outside, but I was clearly right to be careful. Perhaps I could find a way to harvest something edible out in the forests so the others would see some benefit to my little hunts…

We reached the entrance to the central tower, and I bade the captain farewell. Still, I could feel his eyes on me as I walked inside, so I took the side staircase toward the sleeping quarters. I waited out of sight until I heard his boots clomping away before I ran back down, slipping through the main entrance. To my right, I could hear the others in the common room, laughing and playing music by the hearth as they waited for their dinner.

I hope you don't mistake me and think I begrudged these people their simple pleasures. Far from it. Humans always *mean* well. In the end, we're just another animal in the forest, predator and prey, forced to live as best we can. Even if I didn't worship their gods — the Light Mother always more than enough for me — I understood their desire for a simple life. After all, even if we harbor them, we didn't create the shadows.

I hummed as I walked on, reminded of the song the southerners loved to sing so much — *the gods of plenty sowers be, and man just implements to reap.* As different as I was from them, we were all people, some three dozen souls in an old castle, hiding in a nearly fallen kingdom, the law of man still breeding endless shadow. I was no queen to rule these people, no priestess to judge their worth. I just wanted to do *something,* collecting enough light to use the meager power afforded to me.

I passed through the empty meal hall, sneaking into the kitchen. Lura was at the stove making dinner, but she was a northwoman — though not so far north as to have braided her hair — and she knew what I was about, smiling as I passed her.

I ducked into the storerooms, taking the stairs into the giant root cellar. Squeezing behind a pair of wine barrels larger than boulders, I quickly moved a few empty crates and *pushed,* the wall giving way through a hidden door. My mother had shown it to me when the earl still ruled here. It had been used to store wine, something the earl had thankfully drunk as his enemies approached the gates, leaving no need to search the storeroom further.

Entering the secret room, I had to shield my eyes from the brilliant light. In the center of the room, dangling from a dozen old wine bottles I'd hung from the ceiling, was a second sun. The wards I'd etched into the glass had made my light collection manifest, the air between the bottles teeming with dancing orbs. They skittered between the wards, like butterflies made of stars as their light filled the room with warmth.

Beneath the light was an old pool, the dark water glowing in the light as it slowly filled and emptied, the water coming through a narrow channel dug into the wall and fed by the castle's stream. I'd lined the pool with plants from the forest, a dozen different specimens I'd snuck in at night along with soil from the fields. Their leaves gently swayed, the air moving as the castle breathed around me.

Pulling off my shawl and boots, I stepped in the water to get a better look at the wards. The water always shocked me with how cold it was — presumably drawn in here to chill the earl's wine — even colder than the stream outside. Satisfied by the wards, I sat on the far end of the pool, leaving my legs in the water. I closed my eyes, taking a deep breath. When I opened them again, I could see lines of light in the air. Like gold thread, they connected the orbs to the plants, slowly drifting and overlapping as the lights danced through the air.

Another trick of my mother's. Keeping living things nearby ensured the light didn't fade over time, while the lights themselves were bright enough to keep the plants from dying. I hadn't understood when I was a girl, of course. Why would anyone need to hide their lights? Unfortunately, a lifetime of experience had taught me otherwise. The day they'd killed my mother in the capital, I'd run home, grateful her light garden was still hidden in the cupboard.

I shook my head, pinching my brow. This was no time to think of sad things — not that it was easy to think of anything with my chest about to burst with light.

"Thank you, Mema," I whispered, closing my eyes again, the light finally feeling close to the surface.

I breathed out, the dozens of lights I'd collected that afternoon flowing out of me like pollen from a flower. They swirled across the pool like a snowdrift, buzzing around the plants as they slowly drifted higher. That was the moment they would have normally disappeared, flying off to join the sun, but the wards caught them, and the room grew brighter as they joined the storm of spinning lights.

I slumped forward, my head in my hands, feeling at once lighter and heavier. It always took a moment to return to being just myself, my own sliver of the world's light the only thing to fill my soul. I put a hand to my heart, taking another slow breath.

"Well done," I whispered, thanking my body. It wasn't easy to hold all that light, and it was even harder to hold my soul together as it raged inside me.

I stayed that way for a few more breaths, a whirlwind of feelings flitting about now that they were free, the light having pushed them to the fringes of my mind. I tried to take each one in turn, embracing it before I let it go. It felt...*hollow* to be human again, like an empty jar. But jars were beautiful too, and I had to take a moment to appreciate that fact lest I let the shadow in. I was a vessel capable of carrying light, and that was a wondrous thing. It was only when humans became convinced they were something else that their jars cracked, the light spilling out and the shadow creeping in.

Suddenly, a wave of noise came down through the ceiling. Chairs scraping and pots clanging, it seemed the others had come into the hall for dinner. I smiled, listening for a moment to the snippets of voices through the stone, the laughter of the children. After all, this was what I was protecting. Even if these people didn't want me here, I was a part of them and they were a part of me. Even when it held something different, a jar was still a jar.

I stood, stepping from the pool and drying my feet with the edge of my dress as I put my boots on. I carefully watered the plants with a few handfuls of water, and then I turned to go. Perhaps I could find some wild strawberries and grow them here? Soon it would be too cold in the mountains to grow much of anything in the fields, and the people would be wanting for something sweet.

I stopped by the door, taking one last look at the swirling lights. I'd keep collecting, keep striving to build something stronger than a castle wall to keep these people safe. It wasn't much — a hundred orbs dancing between the wards — but for once, it felt like enough.

Mist

Rain pattered gently against the dingy windows of the inn. The village was no more than twenty buildings, but every few minutes, someone would walk by on business of some kind, their hoods pulled over their faces. The rain seemed light, but looking between the houses, the moors had already disappeared into the fog, while the mountains beyond were completely invisible.

I drained my drink, the innkeeper suddenly at my side again to refill it. I'd paid him up front for everything, but he wasn't being stingy with the ale like so many others on my journey. Maybe he could tell from my face I wasn't the type to take advantage of his hospitality. Besides, where I was going, it wasn't exactly like I'd *want* to be drunk…

"So, what brings a young man out this way?" the innkeeper asked as he filled my cup. "Most folks these days head *toward* the city, not away."

Frankly, I was sick of being laughed at when some old bloke at an inn heard why I was heading west. But I'd never been a particularly good liar either, and I hadn't come up with an answer better than the truth.

"Looking for the Castle of Mist," I said as evenly as I could, taking a long drink as I braced for his laughter.

"Aye," was all he said, nodding as he stroked his beard. "Suppose I'll leave you to it, then. You've better things to think on than conversation."

He topped off my drink again and disappeared, slipping into the room behind the bar. I turned and watched him, raising an eyebrow as he left. Perhaps that meant I really *was* getting close. After all, Pa had always said you knew you were close to magic when the locals stopped calling you a liar. In his day, of course, people had feared the castle, whispering instead of laughing as they told tales of people who looked for it and didn't come back.

I drained my cup, leaving a coin for the old man that doubled what

I'd paid him before. A tip for not laughing at me, I suppose. I grabbed my cloak from the peg by the door, taking a deep breath as I stepped out into the rain.

I only earned a few stares through rain-streaked windows as I left town, and as I reached the beginning of the fields, I stopped. For weeks, I'd just walked west, not particularly caring to what degree. After all, when you were searching for something that didn't exist, it didn't much matter where you started. But now that I was close, I had to really *feel* what I was looking for. The legends about the castle were a horribly muddled mess, but they all agreed on one thing — the castle had to let you find it. And for that to happen, it had to think you believed.

I closed my eyes, trying to lose myself in the rain pattering against my hood. The moors seemed to breathe around me, the fog caressing my face like unseen hands. Part of me was afraid, of course. Did I really believe, or did I just *want* to believe? More importantly, after walking hundreds of miles, what was the bloody difference? But as I stood there, I *felt* the castle in my mind. Real or not, it was like the feeling of being watched, the field no longer empty. As I pictured a road before me, its cobblestones full of traffic, my eyes darted beneath their lids, begging me to move before something ran me over.

I opened my eyes, blinking against the rain, to find the fields unchanged. I sighed. Perhaps there was a difference, after all. I tightened my pack, about to start my crossing of the moors, when I froze. In the distance, sticking up through the mountain pass, was a turret. It looked like stone, and yet it wavered in the wind, its walls a ghostly white against the rain-soaked hills. That hadn't been there before, had it?

I rubbed my eyes, but when I looked again, the turret was gone. Still, it had to be the castle. Of all my thousands of pages of research over the years, I suddenly thought of an old Skiyr poem about the place:

"Seen before seeing, its halls beckon in my dreams. Mist made of mist, its fingers coax me through the wild."

It wasn't the most…*lyrical* translation, but I suppose I should have been grateful to be able to read Skiyr at all, seeing as how I'd been left to educate myself. Still, something about that line urged me forward. If you were meant to see the castle before you really *saw* it, then that meant I was nearly there. I was being drawn into the wild, toward everything I'd been hoping for all these years.

And sure enough, as I came around the side of the mountain, there it was. In some ways, it felt like it didn't belong, the castle's walls running right up against the hills. It wasn't like any castle I'd ever seen, either — though, of course, it hadn't been designed by men. Its walls were rounded like flower petals, and they seemed to *roll* like a wave, the wall never forming a straight line. Despite its strange shape, though, I'd never seen a building match the moors so well, the mist simply an extension of the never-ending rain.

I approached it slowly at first, keeping my eyes on the ramparts as if archers would come for me at any moment. But the place was entirely quiet, more like a graveyard than a fortress — which in many ways it was, of course. I'd read one legend that said the goddess Merin built this place, its towers flowing from the last tear she shed as she died. A city of the dead and for the dead, never truly there even as it never went away.

Finally, I reached the castle walls, coming up to a sort of gate. Even as it was made of mist like every other part of the castle, it was…*brighter* somehow, its outline clear against the misty walls. I stared at it for a time, muttering one last prayer as I took a deep breath, plunging into the mist.

For a moment, there was bitter cold, soaking into my bones, filling my veins with ice until I didn't know where I stopped and the mist began. But just as quickly, I was through, suddenly surrounded by a glowing white city. Made from the mist itself, it curled into the air before drifting apart, fleeing into a bright blue sky that was totally at odds with the rainy moor I'd left behind.

I blinked for a moment, my eyes adjusting as I realized where I was. This…was Ten'e'for. Suddenly, I felt eight years old again, running about the city on errands for my father. The legends hadn't offered many clues on what the inside would be like, but I certainly hadn't expected this. Why here? And what did it mean? Ten'e'for was the second place we'd lived — and certainly not the last with Da's constant scamming, moving us about before the city guard caught up.

I started up the street, the blank mist forming into cobblestones at my approach. I stared up at the buildings, the old three-story townhomes like something from a dream. Were these my memories or the castle's? I'd always loved the roofs of the city, the tiles shaped into waves and dragons and a hundred other things, no two buildings alike. But would an eight-year-old remember so much detail? The alleys and the gutters, the streetlights and the shops. Had this place really made such an impression on me? I suppose when you're young, memories form wherever they can, some alchemical combination of age and wonder, the rituals and rhythms of your parents' lives molding your own.

I kept pushing down the street, trying to guide myself as best I could. The streets of Ten'e'for were like a twisted wagon wheel, arcing slowly toward the palace in the center. It felt like I was near my father's shop, but as I walked, shadows began to appear before me. Crossing through the mist, they looked almost like people, caught just out of the corner of your eye. *This,* at least, I'd been warned about. The shadows supposedly couldn't hurt you, though I found myself looking over my shoulder every time one passed behind me. One even looked like a child I remembered, one of my old friends, though her name was lost to me.

Finally, I reached a major intersection, where two of the whirling high streets ran into each other. There was a statue made of mist there, the old queen with her head tilted back, looking at the sky. As I came into the square, the mist swirled about, forming buildings quickly on the other side, as if it hadn't expected me to make it there so soon. But as the far end of the square came into view, I spotted my father's shop. He'd made leather shoes back then, and the sign was in the shape of a cow. He hadn't built the shop himself, of course, just another thing he'd managed to win in his gambling dens, another waystation on our family's fall from grace.

I climbed the steps, the door forming a handle at my approach. I tried looking through the windows, but they were fuzzy, the mist apparently unable to form the glass. I took one last breath, the doorknob cool beneath my fingers. It had to be done. Every story about this place agreed — you took the first person you came upon and asked them directions to the next. And in some cruel twist of fate, it seemed the castle thought reaching Ma required seeing Da first.

I stepped into the shop, the mist sealing around me as if to shut the door. It was a small place, with a tiny foyer leading to the counter. My father — or his shadow — was there behind it, working on what must have been a pair of shoes at his workbench. The entire thing was made of mist, so I couldn't see the boots themselves, though the motions were familiar enough. I'm not sure he'd ever been particularly talented at leatherwork, though he'd allowed the man who'd owned the shop to keep on living upstairs in exchange for lessons. It was a wonder that man never sought revenge, though perhaps it was for my sake. He'd always been plenty nice to me.

"Da," I said, walking up to the counter. The shadow of my father didn't seem to hear me. He just kept right on working, pulling nails from between his lips as he tapped them into the imaginary leather. Was this my father's fate? Spending the afterlife working on shoes he'd never cared for? Or was this just a fragment of my own mind, a reflection of my memories? Perhaps it was a way of understanding what I was seeing. After all, Ten'e'for was the last place we'd been a real family. Either way, I had to press on. Even if this was fake — even if *all* of it was fake, including what I'd really come here for — I couldn't leave now.

"*Da,*" I said again, more forcefully.

The shadow looked up, its hazy face seeming to frown.

"Is that you, my boy? What took you so long?"

"Da, where's Ma?" I asked, ignoring his question.

The shadow shook its head, as if it were struggling to break from whatever dream it was seeing me through.

"Where is my mother?"

"Oh, well, she's at the looms, of course. Not sure where else she'd be this time of day."

I narrowed my eyes. Ma hadn't worked the looms in Ten'e'for. That had been in the capital. Could my memories blur together like that? Could they—

The shadow disappeared, the shop suddenly empty. I cursed, heading for the door, but as I opened it, I found the city gone, the streets of the capital suddenly in their place. I looked up, finding the cow-shaped sign inexplicably missing, the entire face of the shop gone despite my only just leaving it. Still, I knew where I was. This was a place I knew without needing to think, a place where my memories were cursedly clear.

I started up the new street toward the river, the water running quickly in the distance though it was made of mist. This time, the entire place looked fully formed, as if the castle had been rebuilding itself while I was in the shop. There were more shadows on the streets this time, too, though I thankfully didn't recognize any of them. There were too many bad memories in the capital, too many faces I'd prayed I'd never see again.

Eventually, I passed our house, the place looking as leaky as ever from where it sat above the tavern. I pressed on, pointedly ignoring the corner where Da had died. I didn't need to know if his ghost was still there — and frankly didn't care. I had the directions I needed, and I'd find my way without him.

Finally, I reached the water, the giant waterwheels of the looms turning. Even made of mist, they seemed to groan as I remembered them doing, the spokes slapping the water as they were forced back again and again. There were dozens of shadows there, as if their shift had just ended, the spirits coming and going through the wide doors on the building's side.

I sucked in a deep breath, holding it as I pushed through the crowd. The shadows were ice-cold, but I did my best to ignore them, even as it felt like walking through a wall of ghostly water. Inside the factory, it was still bright, the mist letting in the same eerie light as the city outside. For a moment, though, my eyes struggled to focus, unable to find purchase now that I was surrounded by the mist. I moved forward more on instinct than anything, remembering the hundreds of times I'd come there looking for Ma. I'd never forget her workstation. Second to last on the left, she'd worked on the largest loom, carrying giant reels of wool from sunup to sundown.

As I came around the back end of the factory, I finally saw her. Even with her back to me, I knew her in an instant. Her hair, her back, even the way her legs moved, she was forever burned into my mind, more a part of me than myself. My throat tightened, my heart thumping as it threatened to leap out of my chest. I realized then why the legends warned of never wanting to leave. I could have stood there for the rest of my life, looking at her until I turned to mist myself.

You see, it's mothers that make us human. An endless line of Eves, giving us the very thing that makes us real, that makes us more than mist. She may have only been a ghost or a memory, but I realized in that moment that I didn't care. That's how powerful mothers are. Even if she was just some simulacrum, seeing her again was the most exciting thing I'd ever get to do.

"Ma," I said, my mouth suddenly gone dry. How long had I waited for this day? How hard had I searched?

Unlike my father's, her shadow didn't need any coaxing. She looked up right away, her face far clearer than Da's had been. She even had eyes, their beautiful ovals cut into the shadow like onyx, the shape right even if the color wasn't there.

"Hello, dear," she said, smiling. "I've been waiting for you."

The Circle

"Only the Circle brings life," Lord Usil said, silencing the discussion in the court. "To stray is death."

The rabbit king leaned back in his throne, the dried and woven tops of carrots rustling beneath his weight. He took a sip from the royal chalice, the muddled blueberries staining his lips.

Tulzin turned away, sucking his lip under his front teeth. It was all he could do not to tap his paws in frustration. Lord Usil and his bloody traditions! He wanted them all to be content with the burrows, ignoring the fact that it was life outside the tunnels keeping him in luxury. After all, Tulzin had stolen those blueberries himself from the human gardens. Even the king's precious chalice was just a thimble, something humans shoved on their thumbs as they sewed. In reality, the burrow they called home was just a pile of dirt, allowing them to scrape by while they waited for the humans to dole out their deaths.

His sister, Dolki, put a paw on his shoulder. He'd heard her crying at night — knew how keenly she missed mother too — but she still didn't seem to understand. And how could she? She hadn't been there when mother died, hadn't been forced to watch as she bled out on the dry leaves of the gardens, a hunter carrying her away. Dolki almost never left the burrow anymore, too busy with the looms. And now that Lord Usil was sniffing around, hinting at making her his spring mate, she probably didn't want to, either. If only her brother would be quiet and stop ruining her plans, right?

Still, he squeezed her paw, nodding to her as he left the throne room. He couldn't stay mad at Dolki. Even if all this death made a mockery of their way of life, she was the only one he'd ever seen truly live in the values of the Circle. Like the sun itself, Dolki *was* life, making everyone happy, making everything better. For her sake, he'd have to keep trying, have to get the others to see truth before it was too late. Unfortunately, with how stubborn the king was, he probably wouldn't realize he was wrong until every rabbit in the den was dead.

He followed the burrow's ring to the east, taking the first set of stairs to the surface. Stubborn king or not, he still had work to do, and Lord Usil would want to switch from blueberries to strawberries by sunset.

Tulzin undid the clasp on the hatch — the one his father had designed from human hairpins, back in the days when possums and worse had nosed around the burrow as they pleased. Sticking just his nose out, he sniffed the air. It smelled like a fox had passed by in the night, but it was long gone now. He stuck his head out, coming face to face with the castle wall.

Bathed in the blue pre-dawn light, the fortress leapt into the sky, its outer wall at least thirty rabbits tall. For so long, it had seemed unmoving, eternal, the ring around which their burrow lived or died. But it seemed even creatures as ancient as humans were capable of change. They'd been building a new tower on the western side, its stones finally visible above the ramparts. They were making quick progress on it, their sergeants shouting at the workers well into the night. Unfortunately, the humans working so hard could only mean one thing — *war.*

Tulzin crept from the stairwell, shutting the door behind him as he moved into the underbrush. Unfortunately, the strawberries were a good deal harder to get than the other fruits the king liked so much. They were grown inside the castle walls, where the delicate plants wouldn't be killed by the wind off the mountains. There was no one better at infiltrating the castle than Tulzin, but that irony stung a bit when the council kept ignoring his warnings. The message was clear — he could be trusted as First Scout, but not trusted to make decisions for the burrow.

He dashed along the edge of the wall, heading to the east gate. Even though the castle was a circle, it had four entrances, the walkways between them forming a cross. The humans didn't guard the east side as well as the others, seeming to think it was the 'back' of the castle closest to the mountains. It was all the same to rabbits, of course, though it did feel somewhat foolish. If he were an enemy human, he'd just walk around the sides and take the castle there. Not that the humans had ever been at war in his lifetime… What if war made them step up their patrols, keeping the king from his precious fruit? Would the council listen to him then?

Peeking his head around the gate, he found Horsin on guard, the other men on his patrol hiding in the warmth of the guard house. Horsin was a giant of a man, but he didn't exactly seem like the type to know what to do with his size. His eyes were half-closed with drink or sleep — or both — and he stood with his spear on the ground as if to keep himself from falling.

Tulzin dashed past Horsin toward the gardens, crossing the stones in a flash. This was the biggest stretch in the open ground he'd have to cross — and one of the chief reasons not just anyone could be a scout. He reached the first row of herbs, pausing for a moment in the shadows to make sure he hadn't been seen. When things looked clear, he took his sword from his belt — the teeth of the old human key as sharp as ever — clipping off some mint for Dolki. Technically, he wasn't supposed to bring anything back for himself, but if his sister really was going to be the king's mate, she deserved at least this much for her stomach once she got pregnant.

He moved toward the inside of the wall, where the strawberries were sheltered from the wind. But as he passed the water trough, he froze. That was where mother had died. It was almost as if he could still see the bloodstains, still hear her cries piercing the night air. Of course, there was nothing there now, the blood washed away by a winter full of rain. The only thing left were questions, thousands of them popping up like weeds. Why had she left the burrow that night? Why come to the gardens even after he'd helped with all her chores? Her arthritis had grown so bad, there was no way she could have run from a human, probably hadn't even noticed the archer watching from the guard tower.

Tulzin squeezed his eyes shut, forcing the memory from his mind. It would be back, of course — who could forget being forced to watch their mother become a pelt? Still, he had business to be about, and if he didn't keep his wits about him, he'd end up just like her. The hunters were becoming more active lately — though what good pelts were in a human war was anyone's guess.

Tulzin picked the strawberries in a daze. Even as father's voice was in his mind, chiding him, it was hard to order his thoughts.

"Distraction is death to a scout," his father used to say, though the words rang hollow now.

"Everything is death when you're a rabbit," Tulzin whispered to himself.

Why did no one care about the war? They all acted like it was something that only affected the humans, as if rabbits lived separate from the world, as if the Circle didn't like them all. History, of course — and the memory statues in the Great Hall — told a different story. Of the dozens of sculptures, only one remained from the last human war. Carved ten generations earlier, it was the only one made of bone, and it showed a great monster. Shaped like a man, it had teeth like knives and two rabbits clutched in its hands, their faces frozen in terror.

If war didn't matter, why make a statue like that? Why sculpt the rabbits in pain if they were simply meant to obey the Circle? Everyone seemed to think his questions were heresy, but they were like sparks he couldn't put out, weeds growing in his mind and feeding on his pain. Losing mother, his nightmares, the shame burning in his chest as the king ignored him again and again. It all rose in his throat like bile until he wanted to spit it out as a curse on the gods. If nothing mattered, why were they alive? If rabbits weren't meant to care about their fate, why make them feel so much pain?

Doing the clasp on his bag, he turned away from the burrow before he could stop himself. Even if he died, he refused to live with his head underground while the humans waged their war. He needed to know what they were up to, needed to find some way to save his people even if they didn't want him to.

Dropping onto all fours, Tulzin darted through the hedges toward the center of the castle. While it was always dangerous to go too deep into the human lair, he should have at least an hour until the next changing of the guard. The humans did some patrolling, of course, but it was mostly on the walls, and they wouldn't cross the grounds until their shifts were up.

As he came through the inner gates, he stopped, staring at the new tower. It was gigantic. He'd seen its top over the walls, of course, but standing in front of it, it looked like an ancient beast. Made of black stone, the entire thing loomed over him, ready to swallow him up without a second thought. Why build it now? The castle had always been here — at least as long as the rabbits had lived in the burrow — but something was changing. The *humans* were changing, and if they were capable of this…

He swallowed hard, darting from the safety of the inner wall toward the new tower. Luckily, they were still finishing the building's ramparts, so there was no one patrolling from the top, no one to catch him as he disappeared into the darkness of the strange new building.

Despite the black stone, as he came through the doorway, he found the inside wasn't dark at all. The tower had six large windows, high up along the walls, and they lit the ceiling with moonlight. The whole thing wasn't empty except a strange object in the center. Like a tree made of gold, it was covered in runes, its branches choking with dangling amulets, each one glowing in the moonlight. Still, it was oddly small, almost as if it had been made to be his size instead of a human's.

"Strange place to find a rabbit," a voice said from behind him.

Tulzin spun with his blade out, the teeth of his key stopping inches from Laspin's neck. The ancient monk looked as he always had, his burlap robes bunched around the waist from his girth. Tulzin slowly lowered his sword, trying to calm his breathing despite the pounding of his heart.

"Where have you been?" he spat at the monk, the words far sharper than he'd intended.

The monk stepped up to him, squeezing his shoulder.

"I'm sorry about your mother, Tulzin. I was off the mountain, in Liter'kunay. Their queen had a new brood, and they asked me to heal one of the runts. I wish I could have been here."

"It's fine," Tulzin mumbled, looking away even though it was anything but fine. Perhaps the monk couldn't have saved mother's life, but he at least could have prayed for her, could have convinced the king it was his own foolishness that got her killed.

The monk walked up to the golden tree, staring up into its branches.

"I heard about your resolution in the court," the old rabbit said, poking at one of the runes with an old, withered finger.

"So you're here to tell me I'm a fool like all the others?"

"Far from it," the monk said, turning with his hands behind his back. "I quite liked it. Leaving the burrows 'til the war is over? It's bold, and we could use more boldness these days."

"But the Circle…" Tulzin said, trailing off. "I know what they whisper about me. It's…it's *heresy*." There, he'd admitted it to himself, let in the truth he'd been denying. He was a coward, a sinner, a rabbit unfit for the burrows. He wished he was a bunny again, if only so he could flee this place before he brought more shame upon his family.

"Heresy is a funny word," the old hare said, smiling sadly. "Unfortunately, it's the rabbits in silk who use it most."

"You don't agree? Aren't monks supposed to care about the rules?"

"Tulzin Riverstone, when have I ever enforced a single rule in your presence?"

Tulzin felt his ears flush, remembering all the summers he'd spent with the monk — and the things he'd caught him doing, only to be met with laughter at his disobedience.

"No," Laspin said, sitting on the stone and patting the place beside him, "I'm not one for rules. The other orders, perhaps — especially closer to the god mount — but they wear more gold than kings, divorced from the world of real rabbits."

"But the Circle," Tulzin said again, hanging his head as he sat. "Why are we so tied to it if all it brings is death?"

"Death is part of life, little rabbit, but the secret to the Circle isn't to accept death; it's to embrace it."

"Isn't that the same thing?"

"Hardly," Laspin said with a chuckle. However gray the monk's fur had become, he was still the same rabbit who'd taught Tulzin to read rune — even if he still enjoyed teaching too much for his own good. "Acceptance means doing nothing. *Embracing* death means pulling it close, making it your own as you realize its power, its lessons."

"And what lesson is that? That we die alone and lose everything we love?"

"No, my dear boy. That we have but one life, and it's ours to live."

Tulzin looked up, meeting Laspin's eyes. They were starting to turn a light shade of blue, a sign of blindness in any other rabbit. But then, how did the monk still travel from burrow to burrow? He put his paw on Tulzin's shoulder.

"Just look at the humans, child. They die just as we do, and yet, they spend their whole lives building. Beautiful things, awful things. Sometimes I fear it's all the same to them."

The monk glanced back up at the golden tree, the ornaments whirling in the night air.

"What is this place?" Tulzin asked, suddenly afraid.

"A weapon. One of dozens across these mountains. I'm afraid worse things are coming for these lands than a few more hungry hunters. You see, many kinds of life are within the Circle's bounds, but there are still those who would lance it, piercing the Circle with their malice. I'm sorry I was away so long, child, but it's terrible work I'm about tonight."

"I want to help," Tulzin said before he could stop himself, even as father's voice chided him for being rash. If there was something he could do, he would do it.

"You would help me fight fate?" Laspin asked.

Tulzin nodded.

"Then help me up."

The old monk groaned as he stood, but once he was up, he seemed young again.

"Perhaps the gods wanted us to suffer, making us as weak as we are," Laspin said, circling the tree. His finger traced the rune in the bark as if he were counting them. "But they also made us cunning. They gave us these mountains and a place to hide beneath the ground. They gave us the night, when men slumber and dream of their destruction. We're part of the Circle — as all life is — but I would hardly say we're helpless."

He finally stopped, smiling as he stopped underneath one of the lower-hanging ornaments. Shaped like a bird, its golden feathers were sprinkled with lapis lazuli. It looked so real, you'd almost think it was a bird from the forest the humans had somehow turned to metal. And yet…it had a rusted color to it, like it had been dipped in blood. Laspin took a breath, closing his eyes as he plucked the ornament from the tree. The gold came free with a pop as the ground itself began to shake.

The Wall

It never ends. No matter how many monsters I fell, no matter how many arrows I bury in their skulls, it never stops. Every day is the same — months already passed in this station — and yet, we're nothing more than mortar filling the cracks. My shifts blur together, each one spilling into the next. I get what little sleep I can, but I always wake covered in sweat, the creatures haunting my dreams.

They look like lizards, bones protruding at all angles from a snake-like spine, the ridges on their heads sharp and menacing. I ignore the fact that they made themselves from the bones of our dead — such "truths" would help me little as I bury my arrows in the inky blackness bulging from their eyes. Whatever they are, they're no longer men. Even if they've been wrought by our own hand...

Coming out of my rooms, bow on my shoulder, the pageboys rush to greet me, their chipper voices oblivious to the fact I've slept barely half as much as them. Still, I can't blame the lads. I'm the only bowman the king could spare this far west, and if I wasn't here, they'd be the ones fighting the creatures. They'd lost half their number before I arrived, and I'd rather stomach some lost sleep than know their blood was on my hands. Besides, if the west falls, it isn't like the capital will hold. A single brick free from the wall, and we're all doomed.

"Sir," my shield-bearer says as he joins me, fist to chest as if I were his captain.

"Tolas," I say with a nod. "Anything this morning?"

"Quiet, sir. We got the worst of it last night, died down after you left the wall."

We pass the real captain, who nods at me. Despite the reverence the men seem to hold me in, he still manages to appreciate me. A good man, that. There aren't many captains I've known who are humble enough to accept skill in the lower ranks. Still, this castle could humble any man. If the ramparts ever give, it'll be his broadsword swinging until the end. He supposedly has a son and a wife back in Ren'kusi for safekeeping. If any of us live, I hope he does. I hope they're reunited.

We go out into the courtyard, the place transformed in the light of day. If it weren't for the snow, you could almost pretend you were back in the city. There are knots of people everywhere, every soul busy with some task they're desperately trying to complete before the fighting starts again. The cooks are working on a morning stew, stretching out the rations that are coming less and less often up the mountain pass. At least it smells like food, which isn't something I can say about every place I've been stationed.

We walk to the other end, where a half-dozen men are oiling bowstrings, preparing for target practice. I'm trying to train anyone with a half-decent eye, but it's been slow going. So far, only one, Keral, is showing progress, though I can't put him on the wall yet. The fletcher is busy enough replacing the arrows I lose, and it isn't as though trees are in ample supply in these mountains anymore.

I watch until Keral looses his first, only a hair wide of the bullseye.

"Well done," I say, clapping him on the shoulder. I have to force myself, to put on this mask, but I see the impact it has on them. We'll need him when I finally die, need *someone* to take up the mantle. I nod to Tolas. "Keep them shooting, at least ten quivers."

Finally, I go up on the wall, looking down at the battlefield from the night before. There are bones everywhere, fragments of the creatures strewn about, each one bursting into a hundred pieces as it falls. Nothing seems to hold them together but the darkness in their skulls, and without it… Still, all of us know well enough by now that bones can't be trusted. The creatures are strongest when they march south from their homeland, but they can resurrect themselves wherever they find supplies, and it isn't worth leaving them that chance.

To that end, the masons are already hard at work, grinding the bones down into powder. Foot soldiers take it by the bucket to a trough in the middle of the field, stirring it into a thick paste for mortar. They carry the slop to the front lines where the masons are at work on an extra wall, cobbling it together from misshapen mountain stones. It's nothing compared to the main fortress, but it's something. More importantly, it's at least thirty paces away, and every moment we slow the creatures down is another heartbeat for me to draw my bow.

I take the bow from my shoulder. I've already prepared it — there's no sense in leaving my rooms unprepared to fight — but I go through everything once more. To lose a bowstring could be death. To miss a single shot could mean a monster on the wall. I leave nothing to chance, the margins of my work too thin for error. Finally finished, I walk along the ramparts, looking in every direction. There's often little warning of the creatures — a single flash of white amongst the rocks, perhaps — but I take every advantage given me, few they may be. To lose a mason would be disaster.

The wind over the mountains makes me tear up, clearing away the blurriness. I'll need my vision sharp. Still, I can tell my eyes are going. Black flecks float each time I move my eyes, darting across the snow. They fight for my attention, a waste, a distraction I can't afford. In those black lines, though, lies another truth — if by some miracle I survive this place, I'll go home spent, unable to ever fight again.

I could flee, but to what end? I refuse to abandon these boys to die, and besides, where would I go? How long would I really have before the creatures reached me again? It's only ten miles through the pass to Fir'en'dahr, and I hear it isn't much better there. If I run — if any of us do — the entire mountain range could fall within the week. Do the generals know how dire things are here? Do they care? We've been so poorly supplied, it seems more strategy than accident. Still, do they really think themselves safe in the capital, feasting while beasts prowl the darkness?

If only I could— *There.* On our western flank, I barely spot movement by the tree line. A half-dozen of the creatures, likely just the first wave. They seem to test our defenses every morning. They usually die, but they must be able to communicate somehow. By the third wave, they always seem to know what we've changed, adapting their approach. Perhaps they're all the same creature, mere puppets to the inky blackness in their eyes. I ring the bell and flex my hand, forced to wait as I watch them approach. They'll be out of range until they pass the first crags of the cliffside, but at least the masons hear me, grabbing their tools as they run for the wall.

Thankfully, they only come at us from one direction. Even if it's the only grace the gods have seen fit to give us, this pass is well-protected. Set in the shadow of Hound's Tooth Mountain, it sits atop a valley, flanked by steep cliffs on either side. At first, I worried the beasts would scale the sides, but though they've tried — every morning there are fresh bones littering the bottom — it seems even their claws aren't sharp enough to penetrate the sheer rock.

I close my eyes, feeling the direction of the wind against my face, listening to the hum of voices all around me. Some still panic, especially the youngers, but what's the point of fear? I have another hundred yards yet. I hear the thump of boots as the pikemen join me on the wall, the thud of boxes as the men with slings bring up their stones.

I care little anymore for monsters, yet still I fight. I suppose the generals must know this. Even as they grind us into nubs, the will to live is powerful, the desire not to have my bowels ripped out forever motivating. It's like they've simply taken away my soul, bleaching my life of meaning even as I live it. It seems it serves two purposes. Even as I hold their precious wall, I can't think a day ahead, can't plan a way to kill the king, the only true monster in this land.

"Ready!" someone shouts, waking me from my dream. But I'm already drawing my bow, having counted the heartbeats in my wait. The creatures are strangely uniform, their steps perfectly measured against the snow. I release, taking one in the eye at a hundred yards. Perhaps I could shoot earlier, but accuracy is everything. Short of death, these things feel no pain and take no wounds. I draw again and again, felling them. One goes for the new wall, perhaps reporting back even as it meets its end.

Through the first round, I start to sweat under my shirt, but it hardly matters. Even with the winter wind, I'll be soaked through by day's end. A runner shouts, the next wave of monsters already visible from the eastern side of the pass. It never ends. No matter what I do, it never ends. But I'll fight on, holding this pass. Until the end, I'll draw my bow.

An Empty Place

I sat in the pew of the church, looking up at where the stained glass made a splash of color against the stone. Somehow, even with something as constant as the sun, the light seemed to dance, each tiny gemstone rippling in an unseen wind. Perhaps it was the window itself growing unstable, the steeple battered by centuries of winters even as the city grew up around it.

"Amen," everyone said, sitting.

I hurried to join them, thudding down into my seat before I could be caught unaware yet again. The entire service I'd been more like a ghost than a congregant, completely out of step with the rhythms I usually matched so easily. At least they weren't trying to lose me on purpose or anything… The church of my childhood always seemed like they were actively trying to trick people, switching just enough words to out anyone who hadn't been in a while. I still need to do an hour of prep before every high school friend's wedding, scouring the official dogma for the current sayings. Luckily, this place was different — affirming, nuanced, *kind*. The only thing missing was me.

My phone buzzed again as I sat, but I ignored it. Earlier in the service it had jarred me, tricking me into hoping it was a message from someone I no longer deserved to hear from. Now, I knew it for what it was — a group chat, some new and hilarious bit unwinding at breakneck speed, the jokes piling higher until I left the service with fifty-seven messages and no hope of catching up. Instead of making me feel left out, though, it made me feel safe. With my friends, jokes were like the bus — you could always catch the next one.

Still, when I'd received that first buzz, part of me had still hoped it would be her. I'd even slipped my phone from my pocket, hiding it behind my program. I almost never did that. After all, this was the one place where I could force myself to meditate, to live without distraction for a single hour. But this was no normal day. It was Sylvie's birthday. Like some quirk of fate or a lunar holiday rolling through the calendar, it had simply landed on a Sunday. Perhaps I shouldn't have messaged her — *hadn't* messaged her in years — but some combination of the church and the date had clouded my judgment.

I'd been standing on the curb, looking up at the steeple, when I'd noticed the flowers. A dazzling spray of pink, the bed seemed overrun with peonies and foxglove, the color completely out of step with the ancient stone. A single butterfly danced between the petals, drinking up what sweetness it could find before winter descended on the city again. Sylvie had planted those flowers before she left. For me, it was like a cruel joke, but she'd insisted on perennials, afraid no one else in our aging congregation would find the time to plant them otherwise. That was so like her, thinking of everything and everyone — even if it was only in her absence.

Had she known she'd be leaving then? It wasn't long after I heard about her plans, at her birthday dinner, actually, the spring forever tarnished. Back then, though, the season was practically a call to worship, the entire earth adorning itself in beauty for my Persephone. She'd looked the part that night, too, a flower tucked effortlessly into her hair. I hadn't been able to take my eyes off her, the night passing in a blink until she stood, announcing her departure. It seemed her birthday would be her last chance to see her family and friends — myself included.

"I'm sorry I didn't tell you sooner," she'd said in the taxi home, her hand in mine. Her fingers — usually so warm — were clammy, her makeup smeared. Her mother had started crying, which got her crying — which then had gotten basically everyone else in her family crying. She came from a family of criers, a passel of beautiful, wonderful, preposterous artist types who wore everything on their sleeves. I'd always been told off for crying, sent to my room until the "waterworks" were over. I was working on it, of course — knowing my body would keep the score on every unshed tear — but that night, I just sat there numb.

What could I do? We hadn't been dating long. Even if we'd been friends for years — the orbit of her brilliant sun slowly drawing me in — we'd only just aligned. Still, when she'd finally deigned to shine her light on me, I'd felt...*transformed.* She made my whole world brighter, something I'd only ever had my best friend do — or my mother, rest her soul — someone who saw me completely and didn't look away. Someone incredible. Someone good. And now she was leaving. I'd opened my mouth to say something meaningless when she uttered those magic words—

"Come with me."

Could I? Should I? She was leaving for an artist's residency, off to do more amazing things, to brighten other skies with her light. I completely supported her, of course — at least in theory. It would be wrong, selfish even, to deprive the world of someone like her. Obviously, I would have liked for her to stay forever — in this city, this place — but she wasn't a statue, a monument we could all look to for hope. She was like the air itself, and the rest of the world would surely suffocate if they didn't get a taste of her.

But was I part of that story? Like a meteor striking a fortress, I was all stone, blown apart by our contact but rigid nonetheless. She kindly might have called me *solid,* relying on me in a way that maybe really had made her life better, her art more possible. Still, solid or not, I wasn't someone who could just leave.

So I didn't. Sylvie had, and I'd stayed, a shell of my former self, a faint outline of our life together. For the first six months, everyone had treated me like a walking funeral, an egg already cracked. Eventually, though, the sad looks ended. After all, how badly could you feel for someone who'd destroyed their own life? They all *said* they understood, of course. I had a life here, commitments. Who would run the food pantry without me? Who would deliver groceries to my friends when they were sick? Who would teach the local writer's course, molding new creators with my unique brand of confession and mediocrity?

Me. I would. Except, without Sylvie, I didn't have as much to give. I wasn't really there when I was meant to be. I'd focused on the structure of my life and not its contents, letting myself get hollowed out instead of face my fears. It's not that structure isn't important. We have to feel safe sometime, don't we? My therapist lauded me for setting "good boundaries," for deciding what I wanted my life to look like. After so much chaos growing up, so much devastating loss, didn't I deserve to put down roots? And yet, those roots had nothing left to feed, no flower to bring their water to. I was a garden full of annuals, just waiting to wither.

Did I feel safe now? Did I feel whole? I was still a fortress, impenetrable, my walls rebuilt as if the meteor had never struck. I had walls and turrets, all the trappings of something real. But only now, with my drawbridge closed, did I realize it was someone else's castle, designed for dragons I would never slay, adventures I would never have. A *life* that no longer felt like mine.

I felt another buzz in my pocket and sighed, flipping through the program as the pastor read through the announcements. There was the knitting club — which I'd so far avoided joining despite the ample time on my hands — and the spring retreat. I probably wouldn't do any of it, feigning I was busy despite my empty calendar. Still, I was always saying I wanted to knit, so I finally pulled my phone back out, preparing to mark the date. But there, under the time, was the notification. A single, sacred thing.

Sylvie: <3 <3 Talk tonight?

Catching Leaves

"You ever catch a leaf, boy?"

I shifted the broadsword on my back, looking up at the canopy. It seemed the leaves had all changed overnight, the canopy giving up all trace of green in exchange for a flood of orange, red, and yellow, all of it splashing about like it was painted by a god in a drunken stupor. There was nothing like it back south. It was almost like a rebellion against the Great Mother's laws, the usual blues and greens of nature suddenly interrupted.

Although, perhaps that wasn't true… In a way, it was just like home, matching the way the sea changed colors with the weather. Still, like everything else at this castle, nothing was what it seemed. Take Soghar, for instance. The hulking man stood two heads taller than me in his plate, and he certainly didn't look like the kind to run about catching leaves. Some days, it seemed like the only thing he was good for catching was a northern raider on the end of his sword.

"It's very lucky," he said simply, without turning around. He didn't talk much, but already, I could tell he was different from the others. After all, I seemed to be the only squire not being beaten nightly, the other boys appearing with dark bruises on their faces — only hinting at the wounds hidden by their armor.

As the wind curled through the trees, leaves were falling everywhere, dancing downward as they covered the forest floor. One passed near my head, like a drop of gold melting from the Stone Father's forge. I reached for it, but at the last moment, it zig-zagged away, just out of reach. Soghar laughed, no doubt hearing the clink of my plate as I stretched to catch it.

"Harder than it looks, eh? Keep trying; we could use the luck."

Soghar finally stopped at the top of a short rise, leaning against a tree as he scanned the woods. I tried to look with him, though I still wasn't used to the forest. It all looked the same to me, like those intricate blankets they wove in Tan'in Fyr, the pattern inscrutable to anyone but the weaver. Soghar, on the other hand, clearly understood this place. He was always calmer in the woods somehow, unburdened, his footsteps light as he walked around branches I somehow always trampled on.

Apparently satisfied, the giant man sighed, turning back to me with his arms folded. He weighed me for a moment, which made me wriggle in my boots — this look undoubtedly just another test I'd fail. Still, he seemed different today. More thoughtful, more…open.

"Listen, lad," he said, finally tearing his eyes away to scan the woods again — as if something could have possibly sprung up in the last few seconds. "They don't want us telling your lot nothing, but…well, I think it's wrong. You shouldn't go into this kind of fight knowing nothing, and if they're going to put you in my charge, then I say you ought to know."

I'd only been at the castle for a month — and just two weeks under Soghar's command — but as ominous as those words sounded, it did come as a relief in a way, too. Something *was* strange about this castle. The king had snatched almost four dozen of us off the streets of Ptora Bay, forcing us into the mountains on covered wagons.

It wasn't the recruitment that baffled me — we'd all heard the fighting against the northerners was going poorly. But ever since I'd arrived, the knights had seemed off. They were grizzled veterans, sure, but they seemed…scared somehow — when they weren't furious at us, at least. They jumped out of their skins at the slightest surprise, barking orders at us as if we had wool in our ears. All except Soghar…

The older man smiled sadly, nodding to himself as he realized I understood what he meant.

"It's the raiders. They've…changed these past few months. They've always given us trouble, true enough — better fighters than most of our soldiers — but lately, they've found…something, some kind of magic, *dark* magic. I think they've sent you boys up here to buy the king some time, but I'm afraid it'll just get you killed." He pinched his forehead under his helm, the words clearly costing him. "I guess what I'm saying is, if we see anything out here, do yourself a favor and run, alright?"

I looked at my feet, suddenly knocked by a wave of shame. I knew the soldiers at the castle looked down on us, but I'd thought Soghar was different. I wasn't proud of my skills, but they hadn't exactly trained us, either. Half the squad stayed up nights practicing while the other half fell into bed right after dinner, the strength gone from their arms after practicing since sunup. And besides these patrols, we did nothing *but* train. I'd thought Soghar of all people — the one most responsible for our training — could see that.

"It's alright," Soghar said, taking me by the shoulder. I looked back, somehow finding the strength to meet his gaze. I'd never noticed his eyes before — buried beneath his helm as they were — but they were like ice, the same color as the snow on the mountains to the west.

"I'm not saying you're no good, lad. After all, I picked you myself; you…remind me of someone. You *will* be good at this, I swear it. Just promise me, yeah? If we get in a scrape, and you can run, then run."

He held my gaze, my eyes darting between his like they had the time father caught me fooling with his bait. Still, there was something in his eyes that set me at ease. Pride, maybe? He really didn't think me worthless, didn't expect me to swing a sword perfectly after just a month. It reminded me of something my grandfather used to say — *"Only fools and lords pretend they know everything. The wise men are the ones who ask questions."*

"I…promise," I said slowly, unable to resist that stare.

"Good lad," he said, smiling. "Now, come on before we turn to stone." He turned back into the woods, leading me north again.

We continued through the woods, heading down a ravine, the hill choking with scrub oak that grabbed at my boots. I would have thought I'd want to crawl in a hole and hide, but somehow, I stood taller. Even if it wasn't *exactly* praise, the thought that Soghar had chosen me seemed to lift me by the chin, making my plate feel lighter on my shoulders. Still, it came with a new burden, too. I had to earn that respect now. I had to actually learn something so I could become the knight he somehow saw in me.

I scanned the woods carefully as we walked, my mind passing back over our training, desperate to be useful. That morning, we'd been studying maps of the hills surrounding the castle. I'd memorized every line on the parchment but still couldn't seem to make sense of it in the woods. As a city boy, I'd memorized every street in Ptora Bay by the time I was nine, running errands for my father as soon as I could walk. But this? It made no sense. There were no lines to match the maps, no landmarks save for the trees that all looked the same. Until we reached the king's wall, we— Wait…

"Soghar? Why do we patrol *inside* the wall?"

I hadn't seen it yet, but on the coast, the wall was all anyone could talk about. At once a sign of the king's power and his desperation in this war, they said it had taken a thousand mages, the earth groaning as it sent a perfect rim of stone across the northern border. It was supposedly well-guarded, too, with archers every mile. But we were patrolling at least fifty miles south of there, in a place that was supposed to be impenetrable. If it had been only me — a boy clearly in need of training — that would have been one thing, but Soghar was supposed to be one of the best warriors in the king's army. The other youths all talked about him, even their knights wowed by his presence here.

"You mean how do those creatures get past the magic wall?" he asked with a chuckle. He paused again, stooping to look at the ground, poking at what looked like some kind of animal track. When he looked up, he scanned the horizon, his eyes narrowed.

"I grew up here. Before the war. Spent a lot of time in these woods, too, and it's…a strange place. The old-timers always said there was a second woods, a wood *within* the wood. It was something of the spirits, always causing mischief. Kids would disappear, only to be found as men years later, sleeping in a tree. There were mysterious lights at night, odd sounds."

He looked up at me, blinking as if surprised he'd spoken so much. In a way, it *was* strange. Just that morning, I would have been baffled to hear him talk so. But now, something had changed, his trust in me seeming to change us both.

"Anyway," he continued, shaking his head. "I think the northmen found a way into that second wood. We keep finding them further and further south, and if we don't stop them here, a pretty wall won't save the castle. And…well, if they have the spirits on their side, it means the gods chose them, not us. Makes a man think, is all."

He stood again, leading me out of the grove and up the next hill. We were silent after that, the weight of what he said resting on my shoulders. I hadn't thought about the gods much growing up. We had temples to the Great Mother, obviously, but fishermen didn't really have time for prayers. We hung charms in our sails, of course, and made offerings to the Wise Fish, but not much more. Everyone assumed if you were lost in a storm you'd done *something* to anger the gods, but I'd never considered the entire kingdom being judged. The soldiers were always saying that if the wall ever truly fell, the raiders would be in the capital in a week. And what would happen then? What would happen to Ptora Bay, to my mother and father?

I looked up at the trees, resisting the urge to cry. It all just felt so *hopeless.* I could hardly hold my sword, and now I was supposed to fight the gods? If that were really true, we ought to be praying, not patrolling. We ought to—

Soghar put up a hand, trying to stop me, but I ran into him anyway. I was about to apologize when the giant man put a gauntlet over my mouth, putting a finger to his own as he nodded over his shoulder. He crept like a panther behind the nearest tree, looking toward a nearby clearing. I joined him, my heart pounding. There, in the center of a ring of trees, were two men that weren't men. Their skin was a pearly white, and their hands ended in a vicious knot of claws. They didn't seem to be doing anything, though. They stood like statues, their faces tilted up toward the sun, motionless.

Soghar met my eyes, then jutted his chin toward the south, in the direction of the castle. I nodded, preparing to creep back over the leaves when I turned, finding a ghostly white face behind me.

"Run!" Soghar yelled, though I hardly heard it over my own scream. I leapt up, trying to run, but the creature — somehow down on all fours now — lunged, taking me in the ankle with its claws. There was a flash of pain, but then only numbness, the leaves suddenly dripping with blood. I dropped to the ground like a net full of fish, dragging myself against the tree as Soghar fought.

He was like a storm, his sword clanging against the creature's claws. They traded blows as I sat uselessly, my broadsword held limply in my hand. With a wild swing, Soghar took one of the creature's hands, the raider responding with a howl of pain. Suddenly remembering the others, I rolled onto my stomach, looking on in horror as the two from the clearing looked in our direction.

For a moment, they only stared, like they were dreaming. But even with whatever dark magic they were using, weren't they just men? Or had the forest done something to their minds? They let out a roar, rushing over the leaves like a gust of wind. Soghar cursed, not bothering to look as he swung again for the first creature, finally taking it in the neck. Its blood sprayed into the air, golden like the leaves.

Soghar dropped low, his sword in front of him. I recognized it from training, *The Kicking Bull.* Except where I always failed to hold it properly, he took the stance effortlessly, like breathing. But would it be enough to fight both? And what if more came? I had to do something to help, had to— *Smoke!* There were other knights with us in the woods. They'd be too far to hear me shout but close enough to see a signal fire.

I scrambled for the flint in my pack, pulling up my helm so I could see. Just as I did, though, the creatures struck, forcing my eyes wide in horror. Claws darted everywhere, searching for gaps in Soghar's armor. He fought brilliantly, wounding them and blocking as much as he could, but it wasn't enough. The creatures hit him too, forcing him back as they put dents deep into his plate. How long until their claws pushed through, until they wounded him like they had me?

I turned back to the leaves beside me, forcing them into a little pile, my hands shaking. I fumbled with the flint, using my belt knife to scratch against it. Again and again I made sparks, trying to force them into the leaves.

"Please," I whispered, tears coming to my eyes as they blurred the world around me. It felt like a prayer, but to who? Surely the Wise Fish was too far to hear me. Was I praying to the forest? The very trees that had supposedly turned against us? The last spark seemed to float as it left the flint, burying itself in the middle of the leaves. Soon after, a tiny trail of grey smoke curled into the air, rising past the tree.

I stared at it for a moment, the disbelief clouding my mind like the smoke itself, but the grunts and howls of the fighting broke through. Soghar was wounded now, his silver plate marred by blood, a dozen puncture holes in his armor. None of them looked mortal, but he wouldn't last long with wounds like that. There was a vague hold on me from the promise I'd given, but it mattered little now. That had only been a theory, a promise made when I'd thought the man untouchable. I couldn't let him die now, not to mention what would happen to me if he fell.

"Stop!" I shouted, trying to stand with my knife in hand. My ankle wouldn't bear the weight, so I lunged, falling more than jumping in the direction of the closest creature. By some miracle, the creature turned into my knife, golden blood from its chest spraying into my face as we both fell in a heap. Still, it wasn't enough to kill it, and it scrambled on top of me, punching me in the face in its panic, somehow forgetting about its blade-like claws. Terror gripped me too, and I clawed at its eyes with my gauntlets.

"No!" Soghar yelled, but his voice was hazy, like my ears were full of cotton. I kept fighting until another wave of golden blood crashed over me. At first I thought I'd somehow torn the creature's neck, but as I blinked through the blood, I saw a silver blade shining above me, sprouting from the raider's neck. Soghar had little time to help me, though, pulling his sword free as the third monster attacked again.

The dead creature crashed into me, knocking the air from my lungs. It was impossibly heavy, like it was made of stone, and I panicked anew, my pulse throbbing in my head. I couldn't breathe. I was going to die. I kicked like a flounder dragged on deck, finally forcing the creature off of me.

I gasped for breath, my hair sticking to my forehead with a mix of blood and sweat. The day no longer felt cool, the forest suddenly a furnace baking me inside my plate. Still, part of me knew it was a victory I didn't deserve, a bit of luck just like those leaves, the smoke from the fire growing thicker as the fire devoured all the kindling. Or maybe the gods had heard me. Maybe they'd grant me one more prayer…

Bellowing, I grabbed my knife, lunging for the monster's back. Somehow, though, it was ready for me, parrying Soghar's blade even as it turned to swing at me, its fist like a hammer as it connected with my helm. It sent me crashing back into the tree, my skull ringing like a bell. I slumped to the ground, vomiting into the fire. Would it burn me, sitting so close to the flames? Did it matter? Soghar's eyes were wide beneath his helm, the first time I'd seen fear in the old man's gaze.

He roared, coming at the creature like a bear who'd lost its cubs. The blows fell too quickly to follow until, in the span of a heartbeat, the two fell completely still. Soghar's sword was through the creature's neck, a battle cry falling silent on its lips. But it had cost Soghar everything, a claw sprouting from his own neck, a trail of blood already leaking through his beard. Soghar's eyes met mine for a moment as he collapsed, the two of them falling to the ground in a heap, their blood mixing on the leaves.

I wanted to scream, but my throat couldn't make a sound. Instead, I cried, my eyes burning from the sting of blood, though whether it was mine or the creatures I didn't know. I heard shouts — *human* shouts — from somewhere in the woods. I was saved, but too late to save Soghar. I leaned my head back, looking at the sky. If this was what we were up against, why would the gods spare me and not him?

I stared at the slate grey sky, my vision blurring. Above me, the tree was bare save for a single golden leaf. As I watched, the wind picked up, pulling it from its branch. It spun in the air, drifting down through the canopy. It landed in my open hand, its golden color matching the stain on my gauntlet. A lucky leaf. I clutched it in my hand, closing my eyes as I wept.

Exultation

It's rare you see the life you could have chosen. Like paths in a forest, you vaguely know the choice is there at the time, but you can't see it clearly, hidden by the shade of massive trees you don't dare cross. But in those days, on the march with an army through a place I'd once called home, it had become all too frequent. Such was the curse of what I had become…

"Listen," I said to the herdsman kneeling before me, "these men don't follow the Sign of Light. They'll kill you. Just tell them where the others are hidden."

"You follow nothing," the herdsman said, laughing, his face bloodied. He wore the woven leathers of the Kiton, the people my mother had come from. It reminded me of her, of course — and how her son had failed her.

"He doesn't know," I said to the knight at my side, knowing he would understand without actually needing to speak in his tongue.

"Most prisoners don't laugh, Word Witch," he said in his gravelly voice.

I stepped closer to the herdsman, blocking the knight. I knelt down, meeting his eyes.

"Just give him something," I whispered — though the knight didn't speak enough Kiton to eavesdrop. "He'll take your hands next, and your head after if you don't talk. Even if you send him on a lark, I might be able to get you out before he's back."

"Out…" the herdsman said, though he looked sad, the mocking glint gone from his eyes. "There is no out with you people in our lands. There's only fire. Let me have the sword."

I put my hand on his shoulder.

"*Sirash,*" I said in Kiton — *friend* — "there's no need for that."

He spit at my feet.

"You're no friend of mine."

He looked to the knight, speaking Elsond in a heavy accent.

"Sword. I…want sword."

The knight rubbed his forehead, sighing.

"It's not like these bloody sheep herders ever say anything anyway. What a waste."

I backed away, my stomach sinking as the knight unsheathed his sword. The herdsman actually smiled, looking to the east — in the direction of the Stone Home — muttering his prayers as the knight swung, taking off his head. I didn't look away, the nightmares a small price to pay for being a witness.

"We'll just burn the hills, you know," the knight said, looking at me with disdain. "The captain thinks you're useful, Word Witch, but we need results."

I nodded, walking in the other direction while the knight dragged the body to the pyre. The castle — if you could call it that — was buzzing with activity, knights coming back from morning patrol to switch horses and gather supplies. It had been set up in the Long Woods, and it was little more than a giant circle of pikes, though the Elsond were quickly building more permanent structures out of river rock. I'd seen this dance in a hundred places, dragged — occasionally in shackles — behind the army as they razed the countryside.

Why did I keep going? Why not choose the sword like my countrymen? I suppose it goes back to this awful magic, *Exultation,* and the abilities I never asked for.

The gift had come in the night, almost two decades ago. I might not have realized if it weren't for the tinker coming through town. I'd run up to see if he had any of the honey sweets from Piorn, and he'd nearly fallen off his wagon when he heard me speaking in his native tongue. Things had been so different then, our enemies in the west just an afterthought. I'd trained in a monastery until I was of age before they sent me to the Court of the Crane as an ambassador.

Maybe I could have done some good too if the crown had held — signed a treaty or two maybe, resolved a border dispute. But when the emperor was deposed and the Boar Knights took the throne, every hope I'd ever had was finished. All I had left of those times now was a crane branded on the back of my neck, its deep scars hurting most at night, a constant reminder as I laid down to sleep. It was bad luck to kill a Word Witch, apparently, but they'd also never let me forget how far I'd fallen, how little meaning my life had in the end.

Why then, had the gods chosen me for Exultation? I was starting to think it was random. Perhaps the gods doled out their gifts like rain, sprinkling a bit everywhere, and it was *I* who chose them, nurturing a gift I hadn't realized was a choice. Like my mother had said when I left, "you become the things you seek." I had sought to do good, true, but ultimately — if I was honest with myself — I'd been seeking glory too. And look what it had earned me… If life was the people you love, I'd chosen hell, and a thousand miles of marching to go with it.

"You're much too somber for breakfast," Erina said as I walked back into our hut.

"And how would you know a thing like that?" I asked, a grin forcing itself to my face.

The old Elsond woman's eyes were white with cataracts, so at least she hadn't seen the beheading. But if that were the whole story, then how could she possibly know if I was somber or not? I'd always thought she'd been touched by one of the gods — not that she'd ever tell me.

"Because you walk like a mountain troll, stomping around camp."

She hobbled over to me from the stove, cupping my face with a gnarled hand, her skin softer than a feather despite her decades of working. It had been three years with Erina, and sometimes, with my eyes closed, I could have thought her my own grandmother — gods hold her spirit.

"Come," she said, dragging me to the table where she pushed me into a chair with surprising force. "You have to eat if you're going to be so grumpy. Fires need fuel, you know."

"Sure, sure," I said, grabbing a spoon as she poured me her porridge. "You would know, right?"

I laughed as she bopped me on the back of the head. The captain had "stuck" me in a cabin with Erina, thinking it some kind of punishment for us both, the outcast and the kinless woman. But in truth, she was the only light here, the only sign my gift wasn't a curse. I spoke to a hundred knights a day, each one of them milking my gods' tongue for information. Only Erina actually cared for the man behind the magic.

She joined me with her own bowl, and we ate in silence for a while. Our rations weren't much, but I could taste she'd been in the forest again, the knights choosing to ignore her as she wandered beneath the trees, looking for ways to make our food more palatable.

"What's really bothering you?" she asked quietly, the soft kindness of the words slipping past her jokes.

"I don't know," I said, staring into my porridge. "I guess I still find myself wishing I'd taken another path."

"And find yourself in some other castle?" she asked. She shook her head, though she met my eyes. They were sharp, almost as if she could see me through their milky whiteness. "You have to stop punishing yourself, child. You chose the crane, true, but what else could you do? You were just a boy, and now you simply carry on. Besides, your other path could have ended sooner than you think — *El'son'di'ren.*"

The Elsond seemed to think the gods chose your path for you, ensuring either your salvation or destruction. Each time a door closed, they figured, there must have been a chasm on the other side. When it came to fearing death, of course, you only had to be proven right once, but sometimes I felt she must have a point. How many villages had we burned on our journey east? If I hadn't been a Word Witch, maybe I'd be dead already, an arrow sprouting from my chest. I hadn't asked for this war — hadn't asked for this world, frankly — but spending a life regretting a path I'd already chosen wouldn't help me save more lives.

"I have to marinate the rabbit," Erina said, getting up.

"Already? It's morning, just enjoy your porridge."

She clucked her tongue at me, chuckling as she moved about the kitchen.

"Foolish boy. I'm sure someone gifted like you has never seen the inside of a kitchen, but a marinade isn't just some sauce you toss on at the end. It *changes* the meat, like magic except its only tool is time."

"It hardly feels like you're talking about meat anymore," I said, bringing my bowl to the hearth before I kissed her cheek, the one ritual she demanded before my days of butchery.

"Perhaps not so foolish, after all," she whispered, smiling.

I went to leave, putting my cloak back on when she spoke.

"You know, it's the strangest thing. These mushrooms grow in a cave by the river. It's behind the castle, where the guards never patrol. But the cave sounds big, like it runs for miles. I'd swear it runs clear out to the sea."

I froze, my eyes darting outside the hut. Had anyone heard that? It would be treason if they had. It would be a way for me to free the herdsmen, to leave myself before they made me watch them torture another village worth of innocents.

"You should be careful what you say," I said carefully, lowering my voice.

"Why? No one here speaks Ru'nay. I've never said a word that wasn't just for us."

Ru'nay… They'd been a clan within Elsond, off in the mountains, but one I'd heard was long dead. I looked at Erina anew, my eyes wide.

Could I really have lived the past three years without realizing, thinking her just a wonderful old woman the knights had pawned off on me? I suppose I was a fool, never thinking to ask. But to think she'd spent all that time watching out for me, waiting for her chance to free me. To...*redeem* me.

"You'd better go," she said, meeting my eyes as she smiled. "I'm sure you've plenty to do. Maybe so much you won't be back for dinner."

"You won't come with me?" I asked, even as I feared I knew the answer.

"This is my path, child. Just make sure you don't miss yours."

"Thank you," I forced past the lump in my throat, my heart breaking as I realized I would never see her again. By the end of the day I'd be either dead or free, but for the first time in years, I had a chance.

Still, as I walked toward where they kept the prisoners, I realized I finally felt no more regret. In the end, a man can only walk one path. I may not have been a candlemaker like my father. I may have betrayed my oaths and had a crane branded on my neck, but I was still alive. I'd known true kindness, a kindness I could now return. Maybe the gods hadn't chosen me. Maybe Exultation *was* random. But the gods had let me speak Ru'nay; they'd let me spend what I only now realized were the greatest, most terrible years of my life. Wherever I went next, whoever I became, I would be free.

A Peaceful Village

The broken man stumbled down the road, his eyes bleary from the pain. Still, he kept walking. What good would it do to stop? His wounds weren't the kind that would heal on their own, and he needed to find help for his friends too. He knew his name, though, didn't he? His head was clearly rattled from the battle, but it would surely come to him.

The battle… Now that was something he could never forget. The thunder of the horses was still in his ears. The enemy had brought so many more than they'd expected — tens of thousands, and with dragons too. The castle had fallen in an hour. But when he'd woken up, there'd been no one there. Friends, enemies, it didn't matter. Everyone had just…left. The only ones left were the dead and the wounded, the men crying out as crows circled overhead.

Odd, that. Why take a castle if you didn't want to keep it? Perhaps the damage had been too great. The north wall was like a heap of slag, the stone melted from the flames. It wasn't like the castle in Nortur, the diamond-brick strong enough to repel dragon fire. Not that it mattered now. All he could focus on was putting one foot in front of the other. He'd been walking for hours. For all he knew, the wounded men were dead already. Still, he wouldn't stop. *Couldn't* stop. What if he'd been one of those men? What if he couldn't walk for help?

Finally, reaching the top of a small rise, he saw it. *Smoke.* If it hadn't been for the throbbing in his leg, he would have jumped for joy. He spotted a little mountain village, its cook fires sending tendrils of smoke into the air. It was like a ruby on the hillside, every window and door filled with crimson flags, the cloth flapping in the wind from the valley.

How long had he been walking? He'd never seen this village before, and it was hard to imagine a place like this being left by the enemy. Still, how could he feel anything but relief? He leaned against a tree, trying to catch his breath. When his lungs stopped searing from the cool mountain air, he walked on, stumbling toward town.

As he drew closer, he could make out emblems stitched into the banners, each one a radiant golden sun. Was this some kind of feast day? Why the suns, then? It was the middle of winter, nothing at all like the solar festival in Ken-Li'sar. In fact, it was unlike anything he'd ever heard of in his country. Had he somehow walked in the wrong direction, into the hands of the enemy? But the people filling the streets looked just like him — albeit with strange clothing, everything made of fur to fight the mountain chill. Men and women chatted in pockets on every corner, laughter reaching his ears as children ran about.

A half-dozen children broke away from the crowds, running in his direction. The boy in front held a cattail above his head, laughing as the others tried to take it from him. At first, he'd been baffled by the village, but something about those children filled his heart with rage. Couldn't they see him standing there, covered in wounds, his clothing torn? This was no time for celebrating! There were dragons on the plains, the enemy probably already halfway to the capital!

"Have you no shame?!" he bellowed, his lungs searing from the effort. "We're at war and men are dying!"

For a moment, everyone froze, the children's eyes widening as they stared at him. But someone in the village rang a bell, and the children ran off, laughing to themselves again. The adults returned to talking, the square humming with conversation as if he hadn't said anything at all.

He fell to his knees, the exhaustion finally burrowing into his bones. He'd walked as far as he could, and it seemed he'd go no further. These people didn't care — no one did — and his friends at the castle would die of their wounds, cursing his name as they breathed their last. In fact, they would probably lose the war. If this was how much the king's own subjects cared, what hope was there? He—

"You look tired, friend."

He turned toward the voice, finding an old man standing by him. There was a giant bell in his hand — like the kind for calling cattle, only covered in glyphs. Had he rang the bell? Had he made all the villagers ignore him?

"I'm Toryn," the old man said, holding out his hand. "Come, I'll give you something to eat."

There was something soothing about the old man. Suddenly, his wounds seemed to hurt less, and as he took Toryn's hand, he found he had the strength to stand. He followed him through the village, the revelers parting around them as they walked. The bell dinged softly with every step, and the broken man felt his eyes grow heavy. It was almost like sleepwalking, the thudding of his boots on the cobblestones the only thing proving he was still awake.

The village was made up of just a single high street, carved flat from the mountainside, while homes stretched above them on the heights. There was a sort of square in the middle, where more villagers stood around a fountain, eating and drinking as children in their smallclothes jumped about the water despite the cold. Steam rose from it, though, a hot spring, perhaps?

He had no time to find out, the old man coaxing him across the square and into a tavern on the corner. It had an old wooden bar and a roaring fire in the hearth — though it was otherwise empty, every possible patron outside at the festival. Toryn sat him at a table by the windows, practically forcing him into the chair — though it seemed like the only thing keeping him from floating away on the sound of that bell.

Before long, there was a feast before him, the old man darting from the bar and back with a platter full of things. There was a mug of ale, a tray of pretzels, even a jar of eferon pickles, the clump of vegetables swimming in a golden brine. Where had they gotten something like that? He hadn't had them since he left home with the army, what, ten years ago? The broken man took the jar in his hands, holding it like a jewel as it glittered in the light.

"Where did you get this?" he asked, unable to tear his eyes from the pickles as the old man sat, placing his bell on the table between them.

"We have all sorts of things here. You'd be surprised how many boys we get from the south. They all joined up to serve the king, just like you."

He finally looked up, a memory of the king's flag pushing into his mind unbidden. It had been the last thing he'd seen before passing out during the battle, staring up at it as it flapped in the wind, smoldering at the edges as dragon flame scored the field around them.

"My men, they need help. The battle… We have to leave. Surely your people can't stay here. It isn't safe, you—"

"It's alright," Toryn said, squeezing his hand where it gripped the table. "There's time enough for that. Go ahead and eat — you'll need your strength."

"I'm not hungry," he spat, pushing the tray away. "And how can you be? Good men are dying while you celebrate."

The old man smiled — *smiled!* — tearing the end from one of the pretzels as he popped it in his mouth.

"You're certainly spirited — more than most, anyway. Tell me, is the world so small it can only hold one thing? Why begrudge these people their joy? Isn't life both tears *and* laughter? "

"Because…because it's wrong! This is no time for a festival, there's men at the castle who—"

"The castle is gone," Toryn said gently. "Destroyed six months ago. It seems you've walked a long way, friend."

The broken man's head swam, and he had to cling to the table to keep from collapsing into the food. It sounded like there was an ocean in his head, his pulse pounding behind his eyes. But as he heard the ringing of the bell, a sort of stunned calm came over him again.

"You honor your men, soldier. Perhaps it's best I show you first — you won't enjoy your meal without knowing."

Even as he wanted to cry out, to release the rage boiling in his chest, the broken man could only nod. Like a sergeant, Toryn had a way of being obeyed without trying. The old man got up, waving for him to follow as he went to the back of the bar. He opened a door, revealing a sort of alleyway. There was a giant wagon there, the army's crest painted on the side.

"You fight for the king?" the broken man asked, unconsciously reaching for the wood, steadying himself on the king's symbol.

"I always pick a place with a holiday coming up. The people always resist at first, of course — they take the war as seriously as you do — but celebrating *is* important. The people need hope, to stay the narrow path between cynicism and despair."

"Why?"

"Because joy is important, friend, it's how we defeat them. It's how we find the strength to fight."

Toryn opened the back of the wagon, revealing a small forge. It was gold like the bell, its surface covered in the same curving glyphs. Inside, the fire growled with a bluish light, though it didn't feel hot. In fact, it was a wonder a wooden wagon could hold a forge at all. He felt like he could stare into that light forever, could disappear inside its glow.

"You've seen a Wielder's blade?" the old man asked.

He nodded, unable to take his eyes off that light. Who hadn't? Shaped like a cloud, they seemed more light than metal, except they could pierce anything — kill a dragon even, if the knight was skilled enough. Why hadn't they had one at the castle? They'd been left alone, abandoned to their fate. Thinking back, it felt like the castle was just a sacrifice for greater things, the thousand-year-old stones nothing compared to some other jewel the king wanted to preserve.

"Do you know how they're made?"

He shook his head. "I'd assumed the King's Witch did it, some magic from the forest."

"I make them — and a dozen men like me. They're made from the souls of the dead, friend. The souls that want to fight on, anyway."

He met Toryn's eyes. He'd only just noticed their color, a sort of gray like he'd never seen, like mist. He had deep crow's feet on the sides, his beard a stark white beneath his mouth. The broken man looked down at his hands, only just noticing how light they felt. In fact, they were hardly there, the cobblestones visible on the other side.

"I…"

"It was a terrible battle," Toryn said, "though I'm told the south gate held longer than they thought it would."

The south gate… That's where he'd been stationed, where the fighting had been the fiercest. It was a place the dragons couldn't reach, the sky javelins holding them back even as the rest of the castle burned.

"There's one catch," the old man added, coming up beside him, his hand surprisingly strong as it squeezed his shoulder. It felt warm, warmer than an old man's hand should be. "A man must choose with joy. It's the only edge we have over those creatures, the only reason our blades are stronger than those made of darkness. If only we had more…"

"Joy?" he asked. He heard laughter from the high street, a pack of children approaching again. They looked down the alley before running off, their giggles trailing behind them.

"Remember what you fought for," Toryn said. "After all, a man isn't meant to hold the entire world. You had joy once, even if you've found pain now. As old men die, babes take their first steps. You can fight for them still, protect the good in them. You can fight not for revenge but for innocence."

Somehow, the broken man smiled. It wasn't from the power of the bell, though. It was from a memory. Was it real? His mother holding him as a child, spinning him around in the air as he laughed and laughed. The world seemed to spin around him, like he was dancing with his mother again. He closed his eyes, taking a deep breath.

"I'll fight," he finally whispered.

"And you'll win," Toryn said. He opened the door to the forge, the bluish light calling him toward it.

A Bit of Luck

I hurried through the stone halls of the castle, my arms laden with odds and ends. There was a splitting pain in my shoulder — protesting at my burdens, perhaps — but I ignored it, keeping my focus on the walls around me. According to Father, I was too young for pain, but I was twelve, hardly a baby anymore. Besides, it seemed the pain only came on the days I brewed my luck, which was all the more reason to push on, the wicked spirits no doubt trying to stop me. It was six years I'd been brewing my luck potion, which was six years no one *else* had died.

But you didn't save Mother.

I clamped my eyes shut, shaking my head as I banished the voice. The first potion I'd ever brewed had been for her. I'd been so small then, her secret recipe whispered to me on her deathbed. I'd spent the whole week gathering supplies — dashing about the castle, climbing the northern hills, all in an effort to find the perfect brew. But…I'd failed her. Something essential had been missing, and the sickness had carried her off.

"A thing of luck," the Head Mage had said to my father. "Such illnesses are like that. I wish things had been different."

Luck. It seemed to be the only currency the gods truly cared for. Every day at the castle, it seemed something awful happened. Someone on the wall took an arrow through the eye from a group of bandits. A woman in the washrooms scalded her arm while washing the king's linens. A cooper split his thumb hammering a new barrel. In a world marked by chaos, luck was the only thing holding it together, the thin line between each boon and curse.

"Ah!" I shouted — a bit too loud so close to the lord's chambers — stopping as I spotted my next ingredient. In the top corner of the hallway was an old cobweb. I put down my bundle, looking both ways before I carefully climbed the stone, my fingers finding what little cracks there were. When I was at the top, I held on with all my might, carefully twirling the cobweb around a finger before stuffing it in my pocket.

"Larint!" a voice hissed from the other side of the hallway. I winced, quickly dropping down and picking up my bundle. But before I could escape, the head footman, Borik, was looming over me.

"What did I tell you about climbing in the king's chambers?"

"Um…not to? But I saw a cobweb. The maids missed it, and well, I didn't want the king to be angry. I know how he likes his castle clean."

Borik sighed, chuckling.

"Making your luck, then?" he asked.

I nodded, holding my things close to my chest. The other children in the castle feared Borik, but he was nicer than he seemed. Perhaps that was just my luck again, but he did seem to like me — even if he was always watching, always looking for something out of place. Mother had been his favorite maid, after all, so he understood the importance of my work. If I'd only been a bit more talented then, she'd be alive, and there wouldn't *be* any cobwebs in the hallways.

"Well, run along then," he said with a wink. "If I catch you out here again, you'll need more than luck to save you."

I gave him a hasty curtsy, hurrying — but not *running* — toward the northern stairs. Finally free of the castle's gloom, I stood for a moment in the sunshine, taking a deep breath of fresh air. Finally, it was spring. After months of winter, months when half the castle had been wheezing, I could finally stop worrying about illness, fretting over Father and my brothers while they slept. That didn't mean I could grow lax, of course — every season had its dangers! — but after losing Mother how I had, every winter was a pit I couldn't wait to climb over.

Crossing the grounds, I headed for the woods. I eyed the castle's tower as I passed, its golden turrets glowing like a second sun. They said the mages saw everything in the kingdom, so I tried to keep it at my back, hiding my ingredients from view. Like a giant bird cage, the tower was covered in wards that were meant to guard the throne. But what did the king need luck for? He didn't have to do any of the dangerous things everyone else did, and a dozen mages swarmed him every time he got the sniffles. Maybe that meant their potions were just that good, the king overflowing with luck he didn't need. Unfortunately, I'd never know, forced to brew my own in secret.

"Magic isn't a plaything, girl," the Second Mage had said to me once. They all seemed to eye me as I walked about the castle, frowning like they'd eaten something sour. Only Redonsis, the Head Mage, was ever kind. He reminded me of my grandfather. I was only four when Gran'da died, but I remember how he *felt,* his smiles bigger than big, his pockets always full of berries from the forest he liked to share with me. Redonsis was the same. His beard reached down to the floor, and though he was hunched over with age, he seemed to float about the castle.

"Good lass," was all he ever said to me, smiling without a second glance when he passed, no matter what I was doing. Maybe he was simply too old to care, but one time he'd even caught me with my arms full of hollyhock from the gardens, and somehow, he'd smiled even bigger.

"Good lass."

I finally reached the tree line, stepping through a maze of logs and brambles on my way to the stream. Fed by the hills to the north, it was a perfect blue, like the ice they harvested in the caves each winter, or Mother's eyes. "A color of the gods," as Father used to say. It was a pure thing, a holy thing. And perfect for brewing luck…

Reaching the first line of rocks, I dropped my bundle, getting on my hands and knees to reach under the bear boulder. I called it that because it looked like a giant sleeping bear, of course, but it also had the perfect notch under its belly where I could hide my things. Pulling out my cauldron, I carefully filled it with water from the stream before starting a fire, beginning my work.

Brewing luck, you see, is not a simple thing. Just before the water boiled, I stirred in the cobwebs, their translucent threads turning the water a milky white. Next, I dropped in three crabapples with a plunk, adding an extra log to get the cauldron boiling. Each plunk was extremely important. They say magic is about intent, and to do otherwise would be to spit on the gods. After all, the one time I placed the apples in gently, Father sprained his ankle in the stables.

Next, I took out my clump of hay, laying it on a flat rock as I cut it into portions.

"One-and-two-and-three," I counted, cutting equal lengths. One of the king's farmers saved them for me, and they were perfectly golden, kept in a loft through winter. I always shared a little of my luck with him, of course, though it was awfully kind of him to help me. I put the pieces in one by one, holding my breath until I'd added thirty, the water turning brown.

Reaching into the pocket of my apron, I took out the toad I'd stashed there. He tried to wriggle free, but I held on tight, shaking him gently over the water before plopping him in the grass. I would have never dropped him in, of course, but for the potion to work, the toad had to *think* I would. The ounce of toad's freedom was worthless otherwise.

After that, I waited, staring hard into the water. Sometimes, the toad didn't take, and I'd have to start over, wasting a day — and risking calamity as my family went about their business. I always kept an extra jar around, of course, but with something as finicky as luck, I felt safer with a fresh brew.

Slowly, almost imperceptibly, the potion began to change. The brown became less brown, the boil dying down until the pot became a liquid gold, as if the mountain god's cow had made fresh milk. Looking at the sky, I said a prayer of thanks, resisting the urge to dance. After all, magic is serious business. I moved quickly then, hurrying through the rest of the process before the potion cooled.

I pulled out the remaining wood with my tongs, leaving only embers. Then I added the berries and flowers in alphabetical order, the hollyhock going in last. Facing the river, my back to the cauldron, I sang my mother's favorite song. The potion often grew shy at this critical stage, and it was important that it think me busy. As I reached the end of the song, I finally peeked, the golden liquid thickened until it bounced like cream.

Finally.

I took two flasks from my pocket, dipping them in the cauldron until they were full. I wiped the extra from the sides with my hair before tying it in a bun so it could soak up the extra luck. The pain in my neck was at its peak, and I had to grit my teeth at the end, but I wouldn't quit without finishing. I washed everything in the river before stowing it away again, out of sight of the mages — and hopefully the spirits, too.

"Protect us, Mother," I prayed, looking at the mountain's peak through the trees, saying my final lucky words. She'd watched over us so far, but I hoped I made her proud, too. After all, it was her who'd set me on this path, giving me a purpose even as she tore a hole in my heart. "Let us be safe and—"

Ding-dong-ding-dong!

I froze mid-sentence, looking toward the castle. The bells were ringing, which meant something awful must have happened. In an instant, a thousand terrible options flooded my mind — fire, flood, enemies at the gates. It was a good thing I had my luck. It seemed it could never come too soon, misfortune always just a day away, like rain clouds drifting over the mountains. I sprinted toward the sound of the bells, my potion held firmly in my hand. I didn't have a moment to lose.

On Feasting

I wove through the feast, a giant tray of grouse on my shoulder. In a strange way, it reminded me of battle — weaving through the crowds, the cry of voices, my platter like a greasy shield. Luckily, though, in the ways that really mattered, tonight couldn't be further from the war. My heart wasn't pounding, there was no knot in my chest. I wouldn't have to turn away after we won, retching as I watched the crows begin to feast. No, this feast was a *true* victory, one we could share with our enemies. One we could enjoy with no regret.

I finally reached the North King's table, his men shouting and drinking as they toasted one another. They wore their white and blue tabards, the same combination of colors my men had feared for so many years. Tonight, though, it matched my own tunic, the old tan fabric riddled with blue and white stitches I'd begged my wife to add. Their king — the White Boar, as his men called him — eyed me as I approached, though he smiled when he recognized me.

"The Good General!" he roared in his tongue. I'd studied it for years, of course, though it was only now, in peacetime, that it was truly making sense to me.

"I pulled these from the ovens myself," I said, placing the grouse before the king. "I think the cooks would rather be rid of me."

"A man must watch his feasts as he does his battles," the king said, rubbing his hands together. Frankly, I don't think I'd ever heard a phrase I so completely agreed with. He selected two birds at random, ripping chunks from them with his hands. He held them both aloft, bowing his head as he offered them to me. This was a great sign of respect in the northlands, so I took them carefully, chewing each piece before swallowing. It was also, of course, a great means to check for poison — not that I blamed the old boar. There were plenty of men at the feast who'd love nothing more than to kill him, and an entire army that would've liked his head on a pike just one winter ago.

I spared a look over my shoulder for my own king's table. It was just as raucous as the North King's, thronged with knights and choking with ale. At the far end, however, his counselors glared at me. I waved, putting on my best smile. After all, as my father always said, the greatest revenge you can have over your enemies is a laugh. I headed toward them, following an army of serving women who held the rest of the grouse — my own plate hopefully amongst them.

To my eternal satisfaction, the counselors seemed to panic a bit at my approach, their courtly robes unable to hide them. One stared into his wine while another left the table entirely, saying loudly how badly he needed the privy. They may call me a coward behind my back, but just as surely as their new position at the end of the table, they knew the truth — there was a reason the king trusted me, the same reason I had the bear's crest sewn onto my breast. I had won more battles in this war than anyone else in the king's army. I'd held Suna Pass with only a dozen for fourteen days. And even as I'd grown old and fat, I could still lift all three of those wretched men over my head as easily a mother lifts her babe.

I sat, grateful as the first wave of grouse hit me. After all, there's only so much smelling a man can do before he eats. Soon the room was nearly silent, the conversations dying as the men tucked in. After so many years of deprivation, it seemed my men wanted their fill as bad as I did. Across the room, the North King's table had already cleared their first platter. One of his men held it aloft, uncaring as the grease dripped onto his hands. Thankfully, the servants knew their business, and one was already weaving toward them with a fresh one.

I laughed into my grouse, remembering how hard it had been to get anyone to do anything during the war. The last time I'd stayed at the king's castle, it had taken three whole days to have my boots polished. Not that I blame the servants! Everyone was malnourished then, afraid of wasting energy. In every way, it was the opposite of a feast, the entire kingdom groaning beneath the strain of their hunger.

The harvests were fine, of course. My legion had made sure of that, protecting the heartland at all costs. Unfortunately, scarcity is something first created in the mind. The king's advisors — the snakes — had convinced him to hoard his grain. "War is long," they used to say. "A man doesn't win in a single season." And for a while, the king listened to them. He'd locked away ten years' worth of grain, until every beast and bird in our basin was little more than skin and bones.

Our enemies, though, were worse yet. There was only one major battle I'd lost, but it never left my mind. The northmen had attacked at night, glow spores rubbed into their cheeks, shining against their gaunt faces. You'd think we fought the dead themselves, released from the dark one's castle beneath the earth. They'd routed us, breaking through our first line and then the second. I called a retreat, my reputation enough to protect me — unlike some of the other generals at my table, butchers who'd made pointless stands to save face. But as I called the retreat, the so-called barbarians didn't give chase. Instead, they'd raided our storehouses, disappearing back into the mountains with nothing more than food on their backs. It was only then that I'd finally realized — we'd created our enemies just as we'd created our war.

If only I'd noticed sooner. Though, I suppose that's what war does to you. It makes blades of men, narrowing your thoughts until killing is all you're good for. There were always so many things to do, a constant flood of preparations and repairs, all of it binding us with illusions of honor and camaraderie. How were we to think of anything else? At the time, I'd been proud of my tenacity — yet another reason my men had started calling me the Bear. Like a mother guarding her cubs, the only thing more sure than my loyalty was my ferocity.

"To the Bear!" the king roared, standing with his mug in the air.

I almost missed the toast entirely, standing quickly, my men cheering as ale sloshed onto my hand. Some bear I made now. A hibernating one, perhaps? In my old age, it seemed my head was full of dreams.

"To the king!" I called back. "For his wisdom!"

Then I drained my cup, the ale going down all too smoothly. And why shouldn't it? After years of watering it down, replacing pure grain with knob flowers, it tasted as it should again. Two armies' worth of soldiers roared in agreement, finding the bottom of their cups as the serving maids dashed about with pitchers to refill them.

I suppose the king thinks I deserve his thanks. After all, it was I who climbed the mountains to broker our peace. I suppose it was a risk only I'd been willing to take. Not just approaching the enemy during war time, of course, but seeking the White Boar in the winter, crossing passes in the mountains so choked with ice our eyes could see little else. But after all the destruction I had wrought, how could I refuse? Besides, it wasn't really me who won the peace; it was the three dozen barrels of salt pork we'd brought with us. Only by agreeing to end our enemy's starvation could we ever hope to douse their hate.

I sat, nodding my thanks as my own mug was refilled. I returned to my bird. Even as I heard the good-natured chuckles from my men —

"Eats like a bear, he does!" — I was undeterred. This was the best example I could give them. Grappling with a grouse bone, turning the tide against a mountain of potatoes, I was finally leading the only kind of battle worth having. For once, we would have peace. For once, we would feast. For once…we would *live*.

The Bread Seller

I breathed deeply, taking in the smell of the bread. Two dozen loaves in all, they were shaped like fish for the holiday, an entire school of them shoved into the blaze of the oven. Their tiny candy eyes stared up at me, the smell of warm cinnamon sharp against my nose. It was a grounding smell, finally banishing the awful dreams I'd had the night before.

I added another log to the oven, pulling the loaves out on my pallet before starting the next batch. It was a wonder they'd come out so well. After another sleepless night, I'd been like a sleepwalker during prep, my kneading sloppy and my timing off. Thankfully, I didn't always dream about the castle. If I had, I wouldn't have made much of a baker. In fact, I wouldn't have made much of anything at all.

"I'm sorry," I whispered, closing my eyes as I looked up at the ceiling. It was a useless thing, my apologies — given to no one in particular — but I offered them all same. After all, it was a good reminder of how much I had to apologize *for*. I'd soaked my path in blood to get the life I had now, freeing myself with a ladder made of bones. It was a nice lie to be a baker, but it was a lie all the same.

"Sorry I'm late!" Hafen called, sticking his head in at the back door. A breeze followed behind him, cool compared to the heat of the ovens despite the summer weather. In fact, the gardens were full of flowers, blossoming just in time for the festival. When had that happened? Perhaps I needed to get out more…

"I can finish these," he said, pulling on an apron as he came into the kitchen. "You might wanna get out there; the line's nearly down the block."

"Already?" I asked, a pit forming in my stomach. Why couldn't my bread have been more mediocre? I'd moved here hoping to be ignored, to put the past behind me, and now they lined up on holidays! Even having an apprentice was absurd, but as the orders had grown, I'd had a dozen parents a day asking me to take on their children until I caved. I'd had plenty of apprentices in the castle, of course, but that was different. Those were just runts the captain wanted me to keep from dying, learning the sword as quickly as they could. Hafen was a good lad and a solid worker — and he deserved a great deal more than me.

I pulled on my shop apron — the only thing I owned not covered in flour — and took a tray of fish buns with me as I hurried toward the stairs. Coming into the shop, I saw how right Hafen was. There were nearly two dozen people lined up outside, chatting as they waited. It might not seem like much compared to the capital, but in the little town I'd fled to, it was a wealth of customers. These were mountain folk, simple and honest without a wicked bone in their bodies. It was exactly what I'd needed after getting free, though I hadn't expected them to like baked goods so much — or smile as often as they did.

"Morning, Jal," Old Yema said as I let her in. It wasn't a name I'd given her, though she actually seemed to prefer it... The rest thronged in after her, crowding up against the counter. No one queued in this town, though they were so unflinchingly honest, they always let me know who was next in the exact order they'd arrived in outside. I managed to hand Old Yema her order before it all became a blur, each person ordering enough bread for an army, the conversations spilling one into the next as I asked about births and funerals, businesses and crop yields.

Don't get me wrong, I like people well enough. It's just after so many years of them running and screaming at the sight of me, it feels strange, is all. Or perhaps just undeserved… But like the sword fights I used to know so well, conversation, at least, comes easily. I can parry each thrust, moving the conversation forward without letting too many hits under my armor. It would be different if I had to answer their questions honestly, but these are good people, happy people, and they don't question where I came from or who I was before.

"Alright, Jal," one said as she left, "now we got you an apprentice, don't be surprised if a wife is next!"

"Fat chance," I muttered to myself, accepting a fresh tray from Hafen as he came up the stairs. I turned back to the counter, finally finding myself on my last customer. Unfortunately — for a sour old crustacean like me, anyway — it was Lisara. The most beautiful woman in the town by far, I was starting to fear she joined the end of the line each week on purpose. Did she think me handsome? I hardly knew what to think of this face myself, the body too new for me to know whether or not I liked it.

"You're awfully good with them, you know," she said, the warmth of her smile nearly hot enough to bake bread. "I know you haven't been here long, but they don't take to just anybody."

"You flatter me," I said, chuckling, though it sounded more like a cough, my throat suddenly dry. "It's what anyone would do, especially with a bakery to run."

"Hardly. It might come naturally to you, but it isn't easy. You *remember* them, Jal — their children, their quirks, the kind of bread they like. It takes most people a lifetime to learn that much about their neighbors. Either you have an incredible memory, or I'm right, and you *are* good with people."

Memory. A list, fifty names, all given by the witch. Each man memorized, not for his quirks but for his sword. Each man dead to buy my freedom, to have enough magic for another life.

"I suppose my Pa always had me memorizing things," I said, hoping to put an end to the subject. I picked up an extra loaf, about to offer it on the house, when she moved toward the window, peering up the hill. The duchy sat at the top, the cold estate of the king's liege no doubt thronged for the holiday as the townsfolk sought their blessings for the year.

"Do you think the Blue Knight will really show?" Lisara asked as she put her back to the window, crossing her arms, a smile on her lips. I wasn't made of stone, of course. It should have made my heart race to have her look at me like that, but suddenly, I couldn't focus, my blood run cold.

"The Blue Knight?"

A puppet, an imposter, a husk full of dark magic. Had they sensed me here? Could the king find me in this new body?

"Sure," Lisara said, raising an eyebrow. "They say the king is bringing him round the north for all the holidays. Might even pick a new squire if someone's lucky enough."

"Keep your brother far from him," I said, hastily wrapping up her bread — with *two* free loaves to boot. "I'm sorry, but I need to close. I'm not feeling well."

I held out the parcel, forcing a smile on my face even as I had to force the bile down my throat.

"Are you alright?" she asked, taking the bread. "And this is far too much. If you aren't feeling well, I'd be happy to stay. I could—"

"No, no," I said, wiping the sweat from my brow. Why were the ovens so hot today? "I just need to lie down."

I ushered her out, batting away her protests even as the look in her eyes made me wish she'd stay. She was a remarkable woman, the kind you knew you could love right away. She was everything a man could wish for — kind, beautiful, full of light — but whatever I'd become, it was far from the type of man that she deserved.

I shut the door, rushing about the shop as I shuttered all the windows. Still, even in my panic, once everything was locked, I simply stood there, sucking in each breath as if it wouldn't ever reach my lungs.

"Jal?" a quiet voice asked behind me.

Hafen. How could I have forgotten? I couldn't very well close the shop with him in it. Besides, I had to keep him busy. How else could I protect him from the Blue Knight? The boy was a dreamer, a quality I normally admired, but not on a day when it might get him killed.

"Uh…sorry I forgot to tell you, lad," I said, forcing myself to blink. "I figured with the holiday, we could close and do a deep clean. I know it's not much fun with the festival in town, but I'll give you double your normal pay, and I promise you'll be out in time for the dancing. You could meet a lot of pretty girls with a pocket full of coin on a holiday."

I was glad I pushed through with the lie, the crestfallen look on the kid's face finally turning eager. He didn't smile exactly — only a fool would with an entire bakery to clean — but there was a light to his eyes. It had bewildered him at first that I paid him at all — most apprentices received nothing in this town — but he was slowly learning to see the possibilities. I may have been a strange man to bake under, but there were benefits to working for someone with a chest full of witch's gold.

I hurried him down the stairs, giving him a push toward the ovens.

"Go ahead and start raking the ash. I'll be right behind you."

I turned toward my rooms, using every bit of restraint I had left not to run up the stairs. Opening the door, I came face to face with the duchy, the lord's spires staring down at me from the top of the hill. I slammed the shutters, sitting on the windowsill as I had to catch my breath again. Still, it seemed Hafen wasn't the only dreamer in this place. As I looked around the little room above the shop, I wondered if such a place could be fit to share someday. Would a wife mind the cobwebs? Would she begrudge the dingy bed or the cold stone beneath her feet?

I sighed, shaking my head. None of it would matter if they found me. I knelt beside the bed, groping around beneath it until my hand touched wood. I pulled out my trunk, propping open the lid. Even in the darkened room, the scabbard seemed to glow, its jewels sparkling as if lit by their own power. I leaned against the bed, tracing the glyphs with my finger. How long had it been since I'd last held it? Months? Years? It disgusted me how much I liked the way it felt, as if a man could feel nostalgic for a life so full of death.

I let out a deep breath, gritting my teeth as I pried the sapphire from the hilt. It almost seemed to resist, the power of the witch still having some hold over it. Why had I left it on so long? It was my only connection to my old life, true, but what if they got to her and used her power to find me? Besides, could I ever really go back? Could I give up everything I'd sacrificed for my freedom? Strange to think an animal could ever long to return to its cage.

I slipped the stone into my pocket, putting the sword away. I kicked the trunk back under the bed, afraid to even touch it again, afraid of the power it had over me. I would have to find a way to crush the stone, but that would have to wait until Hafen wasn't looking. The last thing I needed was that poor boy begging me to teach him magic or the sword. There was enough magic in baking bread, enough life to be lived without blood on your hands.

Maybe I shouldn't have, but as I walked down the stairs, I felt strangely hopeful. Perhaps without the stone, I'd be free, free to forget my old life and finally put down roots here. If I ignored the stranger's face I wore, maybe I'd even fall in love with a good woman. It wasn't much to wish for, but I'd learned long ago to only wish for simple things. With the bakery around me, such a humble dream felt true. I could be good. I could be someone else. Being a baker was a lie, but it was a good lie. And with a life like mine, what was the difference anyway?

The Ghost

The water was a dull, grey slab, stretching across the bay in the rain. It was interrupted only by the occasional wave, but even those seemed tired, weighed down by the fog, unable to form white caps as they listlessly journeyed toward the shore. The mountains on the other side were barely visible, no fishermen dotting the cape outside the village.

This was the time of year the locals called the Narrowing, when winter seemed to lull everything into submission. People would no doubt be snug by their fires, singing songs by the hearth. But for me, looking down alone from the castle where it sat nestled between the crags, I was finally at peace. There were no living souls to interrupt me, crashing about as their hearts beat madly on.

I left the window, floating through the grand hall toward the kitchens. As I passed the dining room, I was confronted by an image of myself, my family around me, feasting on squab from the forests. We were dressed in holiday regalia, the sun suddenly gone as the hall shone in the glow of candlelight. Time moved strangely in this castle, my dreams only ever interrupted by the front window.

I suppose that's why I looked, after all. Otherwise, I might not have known what year it was — the only marker the changing of the ships the fishermen used. Still, I needed to remind myself, to remember there was life outside the castle, to remember that for most souls, time was a river that never doubled back.

I moved on into the servants' hall, unfazed by what I'd seen in the dining room. When I'd first died, I'd wasted decades staring at my memories, unable to tear myself away from the beauty of my wife's face. But after so many years of calling her name, unable to break the spell, I moved on. She was gone, her spirit whisked off into an afterlife I clearly didn't deserve, leaving only my spirit and the stones, the only thing left of my reign.

I went into the kitchens, finding a cook moving about the cabinets, banging pots and pans around. I drifted above the oven, making my spirit small as I watched. These memories, at least, were soothing to me. They were impossible to place for me, the years after my death blurring together as the castle fell into squalor. She wasn't a cook I knew — which didn't tell me much, as I hadn't known many during my rule — though they'd kept the building running for years once I was gone. I'd had a handful of heirs, of course, though the dynasty had still crumbled, collapsing under its own weight until there was nothing left but memories and fishermen's tales.

As I watched the woman scuttle about, though, I had to wonder. If I didn't know her, were these the castle's memories or mine? More importantly, was there a difference? My father had always said a man and the throne were the same, but if that were true, shouldn't my soul have been freed when they melted mine down for gold? Lately, I'd taken to believing I'd done this to myself, my soul tying itself to this altar of my self-importance. It had taken a millennia to reach that conclusion, of course, but when your spirit is trapped for centuries, you start accepting harder truths. Perhaps I wanted to be this way. Perhaps I wasn't good enough for anything else.

"It's time!" a voice called.

I looked up, seeing a maid at the door. The cook wiped her hands, barely stopping to hang up her apron as she hobbled from the kitchen. I cocked my head, unwinding myself just a little in my hiding place. I'd never seen that memory before, but it was a rarity to have the cooks interrupted in their toil. I followed, floating behind them.

Passing through the wall, I felt a shudder, a sort of coldness passing through me. I was "allowed" to walk the grounds — if there was still some higher power who cared for my entrapment — though it wasn't something I fancied, exactly. I felt...*lighter* outside, like I might float away, the present tense I glanced at through the windows becoming all-encompassing. For a moment, a hundred memories rushed at me at once, the gardens of the castle too alive to have a single identity like a kitchen.

I hurried along, clinging to the memory I'd been following. I could just make out the cook where she walked the path toward the cottages, hurrying behind the maid who'd run to fetch her. I batted away the memories around me, even as I had to grit my teeth to pass my wife smiling by the peonies. Still, I pressed on, unwilling to let go of this thread. When you'd been trapped as long as I had, curiosity itself becomes a rarity. To truly *want* to know implies you have something to do with the information you seek. Perhaps this memory was of as little use to me as the others, but for some reason, I had to know what was waiting on the other side.

The cook followed the maid into a little cabin. The door was painted a fetching pink color, and the garden was full of vegetables. I suppose I hadn't come this way much in life, but I certainly didn't recall any pink doors. Still, I'm glad the cook had a cozy place for herself. The building at least seemed to be in good repair, and smoke drifted lazily from the chimney. Just as quickly, of course, the memory fuzzed, and the current state of the cabin was shown to me — its roof gone, the walls barely hanging on — but I ignored it, rushing into the garden as the dream snapped back before me.

I stuck my head through the window, finding something unexpected. The cook knelt beside a bed, holding a younger woman's hand. Her daughter, maybe? They had the same nose, though the daughter was crying out, her forehead slick with sweat. It seemed she was about to give birth. An even older woman was there beside the maids — a sort of midwife, surely — barking out orders as she wrung out a cool towel for the woman's forehead.

I'd been barred from my wife's chambers when she gave birth, of course, but I'd seen too many centuries of memories to still be stuck on the old ways. In fact, whatever time period this was in, I finally noticed a young man beside the bed, looking nervous as he watched his wife.

I drifted through the room, passing through a few of the memories as I came to perch beside the bed. One woman I collided with stopped where she was, looking about her with an odd look on her face. Another mystery I'd never solve… Some of the memories — even ones like this that took place long after my reign — seem to notice me. But did that mean I was really there? Or had they come partway to me — at least in spirit — to the "present" and its so-called nowness?

No matter. There were too many mysteries to count, let alone solve, so I settled in to watch. For a moment, I was worried the birth would end in tragedy. So many of the memories seemed charged with emotion — something powerful to anchor them. And at one point, the mother's breath growing faint, it seemed it really would. But the midwife was triumphant in the end, and even after rolling the baby in his mother's stomach, the little lad came out just fine, his cheeks rosy and his eyes shut tight against the world. He was alive, he was a person, and he would have a chance to live.

And I…was a person.

That simple truth screamed within my mind. Looking at that babe, it seemed the only thing about me that was ever really true. Kingships, marriage, love and war — they were all just trappings of *doing,* of a life I'd tried to live. But in the beginning, before your titles — before you even have a proper name — you simply *are.* You're born like the sun, shining for no reason other than your own brilliance. You are majestic in your power, your very nature brimming with some holy essence.

I reached out and touched the baby's toes, his wails beginning anew as he no doubt felt the cold of my touch. Still, as I reached for him, a warmth re-entered me, one I hadn't felt in centuries. It was completely disconnected from my memories, my own desire for the life I'd lost. This was beauty for beauty's sake, living without greed.

Suddenly, I felt lighter, but this time, I felt no fear. Unlike when I thought I'd float free of the grounds, there was a sort of *rightness* to my weightlessness. I drifted toward the ceiling and through the roof. I rolled about until I faced the sky, the winter clouds suddenly gone, the sun smiling down on me. For once, I didn't look back to see where I was in relation to the castle. In fact, I didn't look for anything at all. It didn't matter — who I was, who I'd tried to be — none of it meant a thing. In the glow of that light, I simply was. I was free, unbound. And so, I disappeared.